The Crozier Pharaohs

The
Crozier Pharaohs

Gladys Mitchell

Michael Joseph
LONDON

First published in Great Britain by Michael Joseph Ltd
44 Bedford Square, London WC1
1984
Second impression February 1985

British Library Cataloguing in Publication Data

Mitchell, Gladys
The Crozier Pharaohs.
I. Title
823'.912[F]   PR6025.I832

ISBN 0 7181 2472 3

Photo-set by Colset Pte Ltd, Singapore
Printed in Great Britain
by Hollen Street Press, Slough
and bound by
Hunter & Foulis Ltd,
Edinburgh

To Ishma and Crispin

Acknowledgement

The author gives grateful thanks to Dr Monica Still, hon. secretary of the Pharaoh Hounds Club, for her invaluable information regarding these splendid dogs.

Contents

Doggerel

The hounds in this my story
Are overmatched in glory
By those whose names they carry,
Yet here Nile gods may tarry.
Isis, Osiris, falcon-headed Horus,
Nephthys, Anubis, Amon, bay in chorus.
Gods named these hounds, for better or for worse,
For dog, heaven bless us! – god is . . . in reverse.

1

Mainly For Dog-Fanciers

'I've been looking them up while I was in London,' said Laura.

'Friends of yours?' asked Dame Beatrice.

'No. I've never met them.' Perceiving a look of innocent enquiry on her employer's yellow countenance, Laura hastened to add, 'Oh, I see what you mean. In saying I've been looking them up, I was referring to a spot of research I've done into the history of those hounds the Rant sisters told us they keep. Very interesting. Do you know that the breed has remained true to type for more than five thousand years?'

'Dear me! Then the Pharaoh hound must be the oldest domesticated dog in the world. I see that you are bursting with your newly acquired knowledge. Share it with me while I get on with my knitting.'

'What's it supposed to be?' Laura looked critically at the shapeless mess of wool which cascaded from Dame Beatrice's wooden knitting needles.

'Well,' said its creator, regarding her handiwork with toleration, 'it *began* as a pullover, but it seems to have lost its way.'

'Haven't you got a pattern?'

'No. I hoped my innate genius would suffice.'

'Who is the pullover meant to fit?'

'I have no idea. I thought I would knit it and then bestow it when I saw what size it turned out to be.'

'One way of doing things, I suppose.'

'Tell me about these Pharaoh hounds. They will distract my mind from this disastrous attempt at improvisation.'

'Don't worry. I'll take it back to its stitches of origin after dinner and knit it up again to fit Rory. He's the only one of your relations who would be seen dead in that colour. Tell you about the Rant Pharaohs? Right.'

Laura's account of the hobby of the Rant sisters was given with conviction and enthusiasm. The Pharaoh hounds came originally from Egypt, as, with such a name, they could scarcely fail to do. They were the hunting dogs of Egyptian kings and nobles, although there was a bas-relief with hieroglyphics from the reign of Amenemhet the First which indicated that wealthy farmers used the hounds as herd dogs for cattle. The picture showed a man in a rather inadequate lower garment followed by an alert-looking dog. The man, flourishing a stout stick, and the dog, with tail in air, were advancing towards two fighting bulls which had managed to get their horns interlocked. The dog had a collar with two loose ends which reminded Laura (she said) of the bands which eighteenth-century clergymen used to wear. 'I say,' said Laura, breaking off, 'I wouldn't do any more of that knitting until you've let me see to it. The length of it is beginning to make me think of Eternity, a concept I can't absorb.'

'I feel the same about what the astronomers tell us of Outer Space,' said Dame Beatrice, obediently laying aside her knitting.

'Time and Space, and we're back to Einstein, I suppose,' said Laura. 'Do you think jet lag comes into it somewhere?'

'Go on about your visit to London,' said her employer. 'You appear to have filled in your time well.'

'Oh, the Pharaoh hounds, yes. Of course I did see quite a lot of Gavin while I was there.'

'It has always intrigued me that you call your husband by his surname, even to his face.'

'Well, Robert is the rather facetious name which used to be given by students and other semi-educated persons to the bobby on the beat. As you know, Ian is Gavin's other name, but I don't use it for fear of confusing him with my brother. That's all there is to it. As for my researches, there were hieroglyphics with the picture of the farmer, the dog and the bulls and I was given a translation of the name of the dog. It was "Breath of Life of Senbi". I think it must be Breath of Life who has been adopted by the Pharaoh Hound Club as their badge.'

'You appear to have gone deeply into the matter of the man, the hound and the bulls.'

'I managed to get a lot of other information, too. Another of the Pharaoh breed is depicted on the tomb of Antefa the Second, a Pharaoh of the eleventh dynasty. I also came upon a tribute to a hound which was guard dog to a king of the fifth dynasty. He thought so highly of the dog that when it died he commissioned a special coffin from the royal treasury, together with much fine linen, incense and perfumed ointment, and the burial was carried out with all the ceremony due to one of noble birth and high rank.'

'Did the king expect to find the hound waiting to guard him again when he, too, reached the hereafter? One hardly imagines the need for a guard dog after one has gone to join the immortals.'

'It seems that the Pharaoh's main idea was to make the hound acceptable to the jackal-headed god Anubis. Perhaps he thought a hound and a jackal might have something in common. I wrote down the dog's name, but I can't pronounce it and I don't know what it means in English, if it has a meaning. Anyway, the hound guarded in its lifetime the king of Upper and Lower Egypt and I hope it was admitted to Sekhtet Hetes, the land of the happy dead and passed the test of being weighed against the Feather of Righteousness. As for the present-day hounds,' went on Laura, 'if I hadn't got my couple of Dobermanns, I'm dashed if I wouldn't go in for Pharaohs. They come up as being lively, affectionate, intelligent creatures with perfect temperaments, good with children – although that would hardly matter in my case, now that Hamish and Eiladh are grown up and have left home –'

'They might be welcomed by Eiladh's two boys though,'

said Dame Beatrice. 'You were wondering what to give them for Christmas.'

'Today's great thought. I'll see what Eiladh and Tom have to say. You can't just wish a couple of lively young pups on to people, and kids are apt to get bored when the puppy stage is over and responsibility has to be taken to feed and exercise grown dogs.'

'A *couple*, did you say?'

'Certainly. One for each boy. Besides, it's kinder to the hounds. They will have been used to company.'

'Are these Pharaoh hounds very large dogs?'

Laura answered the question in detail. They were what she would call medium-sized. The males would be from twenty-two to twenty-five inches tall, the bitches a little smaller at twenty-one to twenty-four inches.

'Unless you prefer it in centimetres,' said Laura, looking up from her notes.

'No, no. I much prefer our country's ancient measurements. I can see the virtues of the metric system where money and what one may call general arithmetic are concerned, but give me an honest yard of cloth and seventeen hundred and sixty yards to the mile. However, I am interrupting you. What colour are these hounds?'

'Tan, with white markings. A white tip to the tail seems to be an asset, also a white "star", so-called, on the chest is OK. White on the toes is all right and the judges at dog shows will permit a narrow white blaze down the centre of the face. What you *mustn't* have are white flecks on the coat. Pharaohs are smooth-coated dogs. I must say I much prefer that, when it comes to grooming them. These hounds have rather deep-set, amber-coloured eyes. I've copied down the full standard as laid down by the Kennel Club, so if I *do* give a couple to young Nigel and Barry, I know what to look out for. Oh, and characteristic of the breed are their fine large ears. You can see them pricked and erect in all the ancient Egyptian representations. There is a hunting scene in the tomb chapel of Sembi at Meir in Upper

Egypt, and there is a statue in black basalt of an Egyptian hound in the Louvre. Unfortunately its ears have been broken off, but they must have been erect, or that couldn't have happened.

'Another tomb picture I was shown was a hunting scene. It was lively and detailed. There were hounds, deer and a chap with bow and arrows. On the papyrus of Anhai, showing scenes from the land of the happy dead, there are two of the hounds, one on either side of a stream and each is followed by a man. The caption in the book I read says the animals are cattle and that the man is ploughing, but neither looked likely to me. It's true that one of the animals is spotted, but so is the bitch in a copy I saw of a mural in the tomb of' – Laura referred to her notes again – 'in the tomb of Khnumhotep, near Beni Hasan. Fascinating, isn't it?'

'Date?' asked Dame Beatrice, amused by Laura's absorption in her subject matter.

'Don't mock! The date was around 1900 BC, and the artist lived at some time during the twelfth dynasty. What's more, there's a picture in our exhibition catalogue of the Treasures of Tutankhamun. It looks like hounds attacking deer.'

'I must look at the catalogue again. But what has caused you to take so much interest in these hounds that you spent so much time finding out about them while you were in London?'

'The Rant sisters, Bryony and Morpeth, are interesting people, and I'm still wondering what made *them* take such an interest in these hounds, so I thought a bit of research and an application to the hon. sec. of the Pharaoh Hound Club would help me to fathom Bryony and Morpeth. Anyway, I've always been interested in Ancient Egypt and, like a lot of people, superstitious about it. I've got a hunch that something very strange is going to happen in connection with the Rant sisters and these hounds.'

'Your hunches make *me* superstitious, not to say extremely nervous. At any rate, you appear to have immersed yourself in your subject.'

'Meaning you've had enough of it. But it's the same with

everything, isn't it? Once you get involved, you go from strength to strength. Once you get yourself really interested, it's like being in a maze. You pursue this avenue and that, make a number of false assumptions and go back and make a fresh start. Sometimes it must seem to researchers that the maze has neither centre nor exit. You just follow your nose and hope for the best.'

'I am beginning to wonder whether a suggestion I made a short time ago was a wise one.'

'What suggestion would that be? Oh, I know. Christmas presents for the two kids. What is wrong with it? I think it's a red-hot idea if Eiladh and Tom agree. I would much rather give them pedigree animals than cross-breeds or mongrels. Not that I've got anything against either, but, after all, the best is the best and, fortunately for me, the price doesn't matter. I've rather set my heart on these puppies.'

'That is obvious. However, I do have certain misgivings. Do you not think that Nigel and Barry are over-young to be in charge of such valuable and beautiful animals as your Pharaoh hounds?'

'My bet is that in no time the hounds will be looked after by the whole household, although still the nominal property of the boys. Eiladh loves dogs and I'm sure these Pharaohs will interest Tom. Children ought always to have pets, although there must be adequate supervision, of course, and the kids geared to face up to their responsibilities. It's very good training, actually, if it's done properly.'

'Does it not spoil a hound to make too much of a pet of it?'

'Yes, I suppose so, if you intend it to follow its nature and its calling. The Maltese, who have preserved the breed, train them for rabbiting, but it's hardly likely the boys will be allowed to use them for that sort of thing. I see the hounds as pets because of their temperament, and as show dogs because of their beauty and comparative rarity. They have been known in this country only since the early 1930s and then they seem to have disappeared in England until another pair was brought here in 1963 and then eight more came in 1968. Crufts have recognised the breed and America is also taking an interest.'

'How does Malta come into the story?'

'The Phoenicians, those indefatigable travellers and traders, took some of the dogs to Malta from Egypt and, to their great credit, seem to have preserved the breed more or less intact.'

'The Maltese have terriers of their own, have they not?'

'Yes. I wouldn't really want to own one, though. The only terriers I really care about are the lively, gallant little Yorkshires.'

'But how unpatriotic, when Scotland has the West Highland, the Aberdeen and other terriers of its own.'

'Yes, but as Wodehouse points out, our Scottish terriers are all too apt to look like disapproving elders of the kirk. Give me a large deerhound or a tiny Yorkie any day, rather than an Aberdeen or a West Highland or a Cairn. I only wish the Rants would ask us over there to see them – the hounds, I mean. I doubt whether they'd bring them when they come to see us.'

'The sisters Rant are not intending to become commercial breeders, are they?'

'No, but they will have puppies now and then for sale. I shall bespeak a couple from the next litter if all goes well and the family are keen to have them – not that I think there is any doubt about that.'

'I wonder when we shall see the sisters again? Like you, I find them interesting.'

'It sounds as though they are better off without that selfish father of theirs, but, for their own sakes, I wish they would take down his brass plate. They complain that the summer visitors are always bothering them because they think one of them is a doctor.'

'Family sentiment dies hard. Perhaps that is why Bryony leaves their father's brass plate in position.'

'I can't believe she cared tuppence for that conceited, selfish old man.'

'We have only her word for it that he was either conceited or selfish, and he has left his daughters well provided for.'

'Oh, well, RIP then, Dr Rant,' said Laure, closing her note-book and putting it aside. 'All the same, I'm glad he wasn't *my* father. He'd have died earlier if he *had* been, the bullying old so-and-so. Talk about *Daughters and Sons*!'

'I thought we were talking only about daughters.'

'Don't be so difficult. You know perfectly well that I meant the book by Ivy Compton-Burnett, the one about the father who made his living as an author and then found out that one of his daughters was a better writer than he was.'

'Perhaps Morpeth or Bryony would have turned out to be a better doctor than their father. Is that what you mean?'

'Neither had the chance, as far as I can make out. Bryony's chief grievance seems to be that, once they left school, their father kept them at home and never allowed them to train for anything because he needed their services.'

'When we had made their acquaintance I was sufficiently interested in them to look the family up in much the same painstaking way as you appear to have followed in the case of the Pharaoh hounds. Dr Rant seems to have died suddenly and under somewhat mysterious circumstances.'

'They have never referred to anything of that sort. Was there an inquest?'

'Yes, indeed. A verdict of accidental death was brought in. It was decided (largely on Bryony's evidence) that on his wife's death Dr Rant had attempted to drown his sorrows by indulging rather too freely in alcoholic beverages. These did not mix very well with the various tranquillising drugs he was administering to himself. The inference was that he inadvertently took a fatal combination of the two.'

'Sounds thin to me. Much more likely to have been a deliberate suicide, don't you think?'

'There was probably a kindly determination on the part of the coroner and his jury to spare the girls' feelings. Nobody likes to have a suicide in the family. It reflects on the rest of the group.'

'Well, I wish the rest of that particular group would come over here and let me talk to them about Pharaoh hound puppies. There is plenty of time before Christmas, but I should like to get my word in before somebody else wants to have the pick of the litter. Can't we invite Bryony and Morpeth to lunch pretty soon?'

Hearing sounds outside, Dame Beatrice went to the window. She was in time to see a car turn into the drive, an old car and rather a noisy one.

'We may not need to issue an invitation on behalf of the project you have in mind,' she said. 'There is only one car among those owned by our more frequent visitors which makes quite the complaining noise which I hear.'

'Well, I hope you're right and that it is Bryony and Morpeth. We're not expecting anybody, are we? Should it chance to be a patient, there's nothing in the book, so he or she hasn't an appointment. I'll go along and see, shall I?' She joined Dame Beatrice at the window and they saw the car as it turned a bend in the drive. 'Yes, it's the Rants' car, but there is only one woman in it. Looks like Bryony. The passenger is a man. Bit of a cheek of her to bring a stranger here without warning. Oh, dear! I think she *is* bringing a patient. He makes me think of *La Belle Dame Sans Merci*.'

'He looks masculine enough to me,' said Dame Beatrice.

'All I meant was that his hair is long and, while there's no telling at present whether his foot is light, there's not much doubt that his eyes are wild, although I admit I can't see them from here. However, I *can* see that he is making strange gestures.'

'Are your Dobermanns loose? I see that there is a dog in the back of that car. Your pets may not like to have another animal on their territory.'

'George has taken them out for a run in the forest. He'll have them belted up and under control as soon as he reaches the outskirts of the village. Anyway, they wouldn't attack anybody unless the situation looked threatening. This visitor is putting on quite a bit of an act, though. I think I had better loiter in the vicinity, as it were, when he's shown in. He now looks to me less like what I said than something out of the mad-house scene in *The Rake's Progress*, by the way he's mopping and mowing in that front seat.'

'As Lady Boxe said of the Provincial Lady, you are always so well informed,' said Dame Beatrice.

'All very well to laugh. I feel in my bones that this one spells trouble,' said Laura. Dame Beatrice looked thoughtful. She respected Laura's almost uncanny knowledge of what the future might hold and the behaviour of the man in the car had certainly been of a kind to cause remark. It would not be the first time that an ill-wisher had attempted to pass himself off as a patient for psychiatric treatment.

The car was lost to sight as it took the curve which led to the front door but not before both watchers had confirmed their impression that not only was there a dog on the back seat, but that beside the man whose strange gestures had caused Laura so much misgiving was the older of the Rant sisters, who was driving. Of the younger sister there was no sign. It was the first time Dame Beatrice and Laura had not seen them together.

'I'll tell you another thing,' said Laura before she slipped out into the hall. 'I think the Rants are taking big chances by naming those hounds of theirs after the gods and goddesses of Ancient Egypt. That can't bring them anything but bad luck. What is worse, they have even given that Labrador bitch of theirs the name of the goddess of Sekhmet, so that she shan't feel at a disadvantage compared with the hounds. Goodness knows, I'm pretty soft in the head myself where dogs and horses are concerned, but I call that maudlin, don't you? – besides being so utterly unsuitable.'

Before Dame Beatrice could answer, the front-door bell pealed and pealed throughout the fine old house.

'Here we go!' said Laura. She crossed to the door, opened and closed it quietly, and walked down the hall away from the front door, which one of the maids was preparing to open.

2

Eccentric Patient

Out in the hall, but hidden in the shadow cast by the staircase, Laura listened to the exchanges between the caller and the maid.

'Good afternoon, sir. Are you expected?' This was the formula which Laura had impressed upon the servants that they were to use unless they knew and recognised the caller. Dame Beatrice's incursions into cases of murder were ever in Laura's mind, and precautions, in her watch-dog opinion, were always necessary and had more than once been justified.

The caller, who had removed his hat, although he had not yet crossed the threshold, flourished the headgear and then held it over his heart in the way male Olympic athletes do in salute when they pass in the opening procession in front of the seats of honour. He said, handing her the hat, and stepping inside, 'The honourable lady of the house, which is she?'

'I expect you mean Dame Beatrice, sir. Shall I take your stick?'

'No, no, not Beatrice. Wrong play, wrong play! The lady of the house was called Olivia.' He gave the maid his hat, but retained the stick.

'There's no one of that name here, sir.'

'Why, then, I pray you, sweet creature,' he said, 'tell me your own name, that in my orisons it may be remembered.'

'My name is Polly, sir.'

'Let me not burst in ignorance, but tell
Why thy canoniz'd bones, hearséd in death,

Have burst their cerements; why the sepulchre
Wherein we saw thee quietly in-urned,
Have oped his ponderous and marble jaws
To cast thee up again.'

'What name shall I say, sir?'

Instead of answering, the visitor began to carol. He had a resonant, not unpleasing voice. He sang, ' "O, pretty, pretty, pretty Poll! Without disguise, breathing sighs, doting eyes, my constant heart discover." '

Laura decided that it was high time she came forward.

'All right, Polly,' she said. She then addressed the visitor. 'Name, please.'

'My name is Ozymandias, king of kings, but, in this unenlightened day and age, my contemporaries call me Robin Goodfellow.'

'*And* sweet Puck?' asked Laura sardonically.

'You jump to erroneous conclusions. My paternal name is Goodfellow. A misguided mother insisted on having me named Robin.'

'Very well, Mr Goodfellow. Address?'

'Oh, dear me! I am staying at a hotel in a place called Abbots Crozier, but I forget the name of it.'

'Do you want to consult Dame Beatrice? You have no appointment, you know.'

' "What needs complaints, when she a place has with the race of saints?" '

' "She sees no tears, or any tone of thy deep groan she hears," ' returned Laura. 'Well, if you've come all the way from Abbots Crozier, you had better come along to the waiting-room and I will find out whether Dame Beatrice has time to attend to you. Oh, I had better take your walking-stick.'

'No, I need it.'

'Not in here,' said Laura firmly. 'You should have given it to Polly when she took your hat. You came in the Rants' car, I think, and we know them, so perhaps Dame Beatrice will make an exception in your favour and see you without an appointment. This way, then.'

Laura had left Dame Beatrice in the library, but when she returned to it after having removed his stick and parked Goodfellow in the waiting-room, she found the library empty, so she went into the consulting-room. Here she found her employer arranging some roses in a glass vase.

'Name of Goodfellow,' announced Laura. 'Staying in a hotel at Abbots Crozier, but doesn't remember the name of it. Nothing much in that, I suppose. Did the same thing myself once in Paris. Are you willing to see him? He's either a complete crackpot or else he's trying to pose as one, but with what object I can't imagine. *I* think he's playing some game. I don't think the Rant sisters, who seem to have wished him on to us, know a hawk from a handsaw, thanks to a father who wouldn't let them out of his sight, so what about it?'

'By all means show him in. We must not disoblige Bryony and Morpeth.'

'You'll be careful, won't you? I think we may have caught a right one this time. Besides, he wanted to cling on to a stick with a heavy knob at the top. I had to take it away from him.'

'*Take* it away from him?'

'Just a slight bit of wrist-work. He seemed a bit surprised. Said he only kept it by him to scotch snakes.'

'Ah,' said Dame Beatrice, with her reptilian smile, 'and the remark aroused your suspicions. Send him in.'

'I am always seeing angels,' said the caller.

'Well, that is better than seeing devils,' said Dame Beatrice cheerfully.

'I'm not so sure. I think I would feel more at home with devils. Angels have harps. Twang! Twang! Twang! And all those hallelujahs!'

'And all that garlic!' said Dame Beatrice in an absent-minded way.

'I beg your pardon?'

'I was quoting from D. W. Lucas's and F. J. A. Cruso's translation of *The Frogs* of Aristophanes. Do please forgive me. I understand that you are apt at quotations yourself. Please be seated.'

She was accustomed to patients who suffered from delusions, sometimes of grandeur, sometimes of persecution. She was also accustomed to pseudo-patients who had sought a consultation only with the express (although not expressed) intention of murdering her. Time would indicate to which category her present visitor belonged. He had gone into silent communion with himself, it seemed, for, although his lips moved, no sound emerged. She asked solemnly whether it was easy to sing hallelujahs to harp accompaniment and at this he roused himself from his meditations.

'Well, I suppose organ notes would be better,' he said, 'although the Salvation Army do it with tambourines.'

'I thought it was with brass bands. They have some very fine musicians.'

'But not harpists,' he said quickly. 'Harps of gold. It says so in the carol. "From angels bending near the earth to touch their harps of gold." Well, I wish they would go and bend somewhere else. I'm sure *I* don't want them twanging at me. Talking of gold, what are your fees?'

'I have no idea. You must ask my secretary. She will know.'

'Is that the tall woman who showed me in?'

'Yes. Her name is Laura Gavin.'

'Petrarch loved Laura.'

'So we are told.'

'She was too young for love.'

'Oh, I don't know. There used to be a song. I believe it went, "They said we were too young to love. We were not too young at all." Something like that.'

'Angels are ageless and sexless. They tell me they can scarcely be expected to love – not, at any rate, in our sense of the word. Have you ever loved, not one, but many men, passionately, wholeheartedly, spiritually and physically, time and time and time again?'

'I feel I hardly give that impression,' said Dame Beatrice, 'but then, of course, I am a psychiatrist, not a nymphomaniac.'

At this the visitor gave a loud whoop, ran to the door, flung it open and called loudly, 'Come out, come out, wherever you are!'

Laura, who had made it a habit to remain close at hand when Dame Beatrice entertained a more than usually eccentric patient, knocked and came into the room.

'Ah,' said Dame Beatrice, 'am I wanted on the telephone?'

'No. I thought somebody called me.'

'*I* called you,' said Goodfellow, returning to his chair. 'I have a complaint to make in front of a witness. Why am I restricted to a cushioned *chaise* when I expected to lie in luxury on a couch? But first tell me something else. Behold! I am Ozymandias, king of kings. Why did you wrest my sceptre from me?'

'Ozymandias may have had a sceptre,' said Laura, 'but it is just as likely that his symbols of royalty were a crook and a flail. None of the three would be allowed in the consulting-room, neither are walking-sticks, umbrellas, a conductor's baton or a Boy Scout's staff. I could add to the list, but no doubt you get the drift.' At a nod from Dame Beatrice, she seated herself between her employer and the patient and flipped open her notebook. Goodfellow looked sadly at Dame Beatrice.

' "But, save his good broadsword, he weapons had none," ' he said plaintively.

'But you don't need weapons here,' said Dame Beatrice. 'There is nothing to be afraid of – except your own sins.'

'I am not afraid with any amazement. The angels are always talking to me about sins. What do *you* think?'

'He that one sin in conscience keeps
  When he to quiet goes –'

'But I haven't got twenty mortal foes. You need twenty mortal foes to sleep among. It says so.'

'Poetic exaggeration.'

'I don't think I'll stay any longer. I wish you well.' He rose from his chair.

'Give our love to the angels,' murmured Laura, going to the bell to notify the maid that the visitor was leaving. She accompanied him into the hall, took his hat from Polly, resurrected his heavy walking-stick and escorted him to the front door. She watched him get into the car. The last she heard was his voice raised in song, inspired, no doubt, by the driver's surname. ' "So we'll rant and we'll roar, like true British sailors. We'll rant and we'll roar all on the high seas." '

The woman in the driver's seat waved to Laura. Laura waved back, closed the door and returned to Dame Beatrice.

'Funny sort of cuss,' she said. 'I'm sorry the Rants have got themselves mixed up with him.'

'Let us hope it is but a passing phase. If he is staying at a hotel, doubtless he is only a bird of passage. Now, it will take that car almost an hour to get back to Abbots Crozier. Get Morpeth on the telephone. Find out what she knows about our caller.'

'Caller? Yes, he hardly turned out to be a patient, did he? I wonder what his object was in coming here and talking all that rot?'

'You do not think that the rather inexperienced sisters sent him to us simply because they thought he was in need of my help?'

'Could be just that, I suppose, but I think there is more to it than that. I think this Goodfellow has scared them pretty badly and that they are asking help for themselves rather than for him.'

'An interesting conjecture. Well, find out what Morpeth has to say.'

Morpeth was contrite and apologised several times during the telephone conversation.

'I *told* Bryony we ought to have asked you before we sent

you this rather awful man. He seems quite strange in the head. Bryony disagreed because she said she thought that, if we told you how crazy he is, you wouldn't want to have anything to do with him. We've had an awfully trying time the last few weeks. First there was Susan – you know, the woman who wished herself on us last year as unpaid kennel-maid. She asked for the job and we took her on, but now she keeps wanting us to get rid of poor Sekhmet.'

'That Labrador you told us about?'

'Yes, the poor, harmless, friendly creature. We wouldn't dream of getting rid of her, but Susan won't give up arguing.'

'Sack her if she's a nuisance. After all, it's your dog, not hers.'

'She says that, when Sekhmet comes into season, there is always the chance of a *mésalliance* with one of the Pharaohs, but I don't see how that would matter. We would have to sell the puppies cheap or even give them away to good homes, that's all, but Susan says an accidental mating could contaminate the Pharaoh stock. I can't see how. It might be different if Isis or Nephthys had a litter by a male Labrador, but there's no chance of that. We're much too careful. What do *you* think?'

'I haven't a clue, except that I wouldn't allow Susan to rule the roost.'

'She isn't our only trouble. We think we've got a prowler.'

'That isn't a pleasant thought. What about going to the police?'

'I don't think we've enough to go on.'

'I don't know so much. Those hounds of yours must be pretty valuable. You don't want somebody poaching one of them and going off with it.'

'I don't think there's much chance of that. We think it's *us* he's spying on and that, when he gets the opportunity, he will do us some harm.'

'What makes you think so?'

'He comes and taps on windows and then runs away. We've never seen him face to face, only as a shadow in the garden.'

'What makes you afraid he means mischief?'

'We think he may be from the unlucky family of those patients who died when our father was still alive. It's left some nasty feeling in the village and there was a bit of a demonstration at father's funeral.'

'I certainly think that for you to go to the police is the answer.'

'And have my father's bad luck – because that is all it was – discussed all over again in open court? We'd rather die. Then, as though that wasn't enough, this madman comes along and insists that we are doctors and must treat him. I'll say again how terribly sorry we are to have burdened you with him, but he frightened us so much that Bryony said he must be mad and that Dame Beatrice was our only hope. I know we ought to have rung up and asked before Bryony brought him over to you, but – is she willing to treat him? He seemed very ready to go to her.'

'I should have thought there was somebody nearer to you. Anyway, he didn't stay long. I saw that Bryony had one of the hounds in the back of the car. Was that a precautionary measure?'

'Yes, of course. We didn't trust the man, but nobody would touch either of us while we were under the protection of Osiris.'

Laura rightly took it that Osiris was the guardian hound and not the god in person, although, as she said to Dame Beatrice later, with Morpeth you never knew.

'Very wise to take him along,' she said over the telephone, 'I suppose this man couldn't also be your prowler?'

'Oh, good gracious, no! At least, I do hope not. I'm sure the prowler is a villager who bears us a grudge because of father.'

'Doctors make mistakes at times, but nobody thinks they intend to harm a patient.'

'We're not liked by the villagers. They don't like the hounds, either.'

'Well, if your prowler does any more window-tapping, you take my advice and call the police.'

'What news from the hills?' asked Dame Beatrice when Laura went back to her. Laura reported the conversation and it turned on to the subject of doctors as murderers. The names of Crippen, Buck Ruxton, Palmer, Pritchard and Lamson came up. Laura also spoke of a French physician born in Lyons, who, later, practised in Paris and was suspected of murdering wealthy women patients for their money or to cash in on life assurances he had taken out in their names.

The evergreen mystery of Charles Bravo's death in 1877 at The Priory, a house in Balham, came into the conversation, although, as Dame Beatrice pointed out, if Charles Bravo was murdered by the administering of poison – tartar emetic among other things was mentioned – it was unlikely, on the evidence provided, to have been Dr Gully who was the criminal.

'And, of course, Thomas Neill Cream studied medicine,' said Laura, 'and gave unfortunate girls drinks with "white stuff" in them. Then there was the Polish barber–surgeon Klosowski, who called himself George Chapman after he had parted from a young woman of that name. You don't suppose somebody in the village got a bit fanciful and imaginative and spread it about that the Rants' father knocked off a patient or two for gain, do you?'

'I do not think much gain could accrue to him from cottagers. These morbid speculations do not become you and are extremely far-fetched.'

'Their father seems to have been anything but a poor man when he died, and that doesn't sound much like a village GP,' argued Laura.

'Perhaps the mother left money.'

'Yes,' said Laura. 'We never hear anything about the mother, do we?'

'She may have died when the girls were very young.'

Laura agreed and the conversation drifted into other

channels, but, after supper, as they were settling down to the business of working on Dame Beatrice's memoirs – a project masterminded in a sense by Laura, since she had suggested it and had insisted that it would be an interesting and valuable addition to the already published volumes of Dame Beatrice's case notes – Laura asked whether Dame Beatrice had come to any further conclusions with regard to Goodfellow's visit.

'Morpeth said on the phone that he made no bones about coming all this way. However, you don't think he is a case in need of psychiatry, do you? He is playing some game, you think.'

'Most people are in need of psychiatry of one sort or another. Some people find what they need by attending church, others by confiding in sympathetic friends. Some find it in their work, others in strenuous sport. These things all minister to minds diseased and that means most minds.'

'Good heavens! Is *that* why I've always been hooked on swimming?'

'To return to a subject from which we appear to have deviated, I think the reason Mr Goodfellow called is that he was anxious to have a good look at us,' said Dame Beatrice, 'and possibly, as you would say, to size us up.'

'But why?'

'That is the question.'

'It's one to which you think you know the answer, isn't it, though?'

'No, I do not know the answer. I do know, however, that he is not mentally disturbed in the sense that he would have us believe. What he really has on his mind I cannot say.'

'You don't think – I know it's a very long shot – that the Rants had any reason of their own, except that he scared them, for bringing him here? Bryony, in particular, could be a bit cagey, I think.'

'What makes you suggest that?'

'Morpeth admitted that they know you don't see people – patients, I mean – without an appointment. If he had come on his own and if we had not recognised the car and Bryony in it, you wouldn't have given him an interview, would you?'

'Probably not.'

'Emphatically not, because I should have sent him to the right-about as soon as I heard him talking all that rubbish to Polly at the front door.'

'Dear me! How high-handed you have become!'

'I'll tell you another thing,' said Laura. 'This business of a prowler at Crozier Lodge. Do you think he can be in league with that Susan woman who, apparently, works for the Rants for nothing? It was very odd, the way she suddenly walked herself into their lives.'

'During their father's lifetime she would have had no place at Crozier Lodge. There were no Pharaohs there then. Bryony told me that, when Dr Rant died, the sisters spent a long time deciding whether or not to stay on at the Lodge. The house and its grounds seemed too large for the two of them. The Pharaohs were a way of justifying their staying on. Whatever they say about her, Susan's advent must have been a godsend. Your own acquaintance with the Rants began under far more unusual circumstances than did Susan's, if you remember.'

'I was a witness to the result of a car accident, that's all. You know the story. A lorry had pushed the Rants' car off the road and into a ditch. It happened sufficiently near here for me to give them a chance to telephone a garage from here and give them a cuppa. They were pretty badly shaken up, you know. Returning to this question of a prowler, I've told Morpeth that the thing to do is to tell the police.'

'Or set the hounds on him. He would scarcely be prepared to face half a dozen of them. I wonder that two otherwise unprotected women have not thought of one or other of these alternatives for themselves.'

'If the prowler is in league with that Susan woman, the hounds wouldn't be much good. She has probably got them where she wants them by now. After all, she's the kennel-maid.'

'I see no reason why you should suspect her.'

'I always suspect people who do something for nothing.'

'But that does not apply to Susan. She is provided with food, with a task which, no doubt, she finds agreeable and, more than all, with the companionship of other women. She may feel a real need for that, don't you think?'

'Perhaps. Anyway, I don't trust her.'

'But you have never even met her,' said Dame Beatrice reasonably.

'I know, but something about that set-up stinks.'

'The foul odour may not emanate from Susan.'

'I'd like a chance to size her up, but, as we are never asked to visit Crozier Lodge, I don't suppose I shall get one.'

3

A Thief in the Dog-Watches

Abbots Bay and Abbots Crozier were sometimes referred to as
twin villages, but it would be more nearly true to say that they
were mother and daughter.

When seaside holidays became fashionable, people were
not slow to discover the charms of Abbots Bay, but it was
situated between two headlands. As it could not expand east
or west, the village of Abbots Crozier came into being on the
clifftop and a cliff railway was built for the convenience of
visitors. Hotels sprang up, the cottagers and other house-
holders took in holidaymakers and both villages flourished.

The coast was rock-bound and the sea treacherous, so at
Abbots Bay a large sea-water pool was constructed so that
bathing was safe at any state of the tide, the rise and fall of
which kept the pool clean.

Abbots Crozier had its own attractions. Its hotel windows
commanded wide views of the sea and the moors and there
were pleasant walks to be had in the upland air and along the
banks of the little river which, when it reached the top of the
cliffs, foamed, churned and rushed downhill to meet the sea.
It bypassed most of the residential part of Abbots Crozier, but
cut its way through the middle of the village of Abbots Bay,
which it had been known on one occasion to devastate with
severe floods.

Susan's cottage was almost at sea level. The house occupied
by Bryony and Morpeth Rant was on the hilltop hard by the
rest of the village on the cliffs. Justifiably had Goodfellow
complained of the thoughtlessness of parents who saddled

their off-spring with baptismal names likely to embarrass them
when they grew older. Morpeth's name was a case in point.
Between the births of the two girls their mother had become
an addict of folk songs (of the Cecil Sharp kind) and the old
country dance tunes. The Morpeth Rant had been one of her
favourites and the unfortunate Morpeth suffered in consequence.

Whenever possible she would sign herself as M. Rant, and
she envied her sister the name Bryony, although Bryony herself had no liking for it. It had been her father's choice. She
had been born with black hair and he had exclaimed, 'Black
bryony! I saw some in the woods alongside the river yesterday.'

'The berries are red,' said her mother.

'No matter. The plant is called black bryony. I like the
name, so Bryony let the child be called.'

When their mother died, the girls were nineteen and
twenty-two respectively. Morpeth became her father's receptionist. Bryony, with the aid of a charwoman, ran the house
and drove the car when Dr Rant made his round of afternoon
visits to patients who were too infirm or too self-important to
attend his surgery. Both girls disliked their father and, to
compensate for this, had never taken down his brass plate or
disposed of his effects except for his clothes.

They kept the brass plate brightly polished and although
they banished to the garage lumber room his case of surgical
instruments, together with the black bag and its contents
which he had carried with him on his rounds, they had not
parted with them.

From the time when Laura had rescued them after their car
accident, they had been occasional but welcome visitors to the
Stone House, although neither Dame Beatrice nor Laura had
ever been invited to brave the Pharaoh hounds at Crozier
Lodge. This was largely because the sisters had not regarded
their hospitality as coming up to Stone House standards. Laura
guessed that this was the reason, but there was nothing she
could do about it.

'It stands to reason,' said Bryony, when the matter had came up for discussion once again recently, 'that, living in that lovely old house and having maids and a French chef, Dame Beatrice would think that our accommodation and cookery were derived from the backwoods and ourselves smelling strongly of dog.'

'They keep dogs themselves,' Morpeth had pointed out.

'Only two.'

'I don't see anything wrong with our house.'

'Not for us, perhaps, but those two are used to better things, and, anyway, our cookery would not be up to their standard. Again, we spend so much time with the hounds that there is little left to spend in entertaining visitors.'

'We've got Susan now. With her help with the hounds, it seems strange and uncouth not to return hospitality.'

'I am sure Dame Beatrice will like it better the way things are. We do not have to go to the Stone House every time we are invited. In any case, there is a limit to the number of times we can leave Susan to cope with seven dogs. We don't want to lose her, do we?'

'I don't believe she would leave us. She asked to come here. Where else would she go to find something she really wanted to do? There are no other kennels near here where seven beautiful dogs are kept.'

'Seven? You can hardly count Sekhmet. Anyway, as for Susan, it would be awful if she elected to leave us. We must see to it that she has no reason to do so. She knows the hounds and they know her, and that is what really matters.'

'I should like to know Laura Gavin better,' said Morpeth.

'Let us hope she feels the same about you, but I doubt it. She has Dame Beatrice, a husband, a son and a daughter. Why should she want more? Come along. It's feeding time.'

All the hounds in residence at Crozier Lodge were named after the gods and goddesses of Ancient Egypt. There were six of them. The dogs were called Osiris, Horus, Amon and Anubis. The two bitches were Isis and Nephthys. Then there was Sekhmet, the liver-coloured Labrador whom the tender-hearted Morpeth had bought from a pet shop in Axehead, the nearest town and the place where the sisters did some of their shopping.

The male hounds took little or no interest in Sekhmet. It was as though they were as conscious of class distinctions as are many human beings. They never rounded on her or ganged up against her, but this was partly because she was never allowed to run with them. The other two bitches tolerated her, for all three were allowed a run in the grounds together, but her heart was set upon fraternising with the dogs and her nose was always against the heavy, high, wire-netting fence which surrounded the spacious stable yard in which the dogs exercised themselves when they were not being taken for their daily run on the moor.

'I believe she thinks she *is* a dog,' said Morpeth.

'Poor cow,' said Bryony. 'Don't you remember how we always wished we were boys when we were young? If we had been, father would have sent us to college and we would have made a place for ourselves in the world.'

'We shall do that with the Pharaoh hounds,' said Morpeth.

The stables had been converted into cubicles, so that each of the six Pharaohs had his or her own domain. Each of the three handlers had her own couple to take on to the moor for exercise. Bryony took Osiris and Horus, Morpeth had Amon and Anubis, and Susan was responsible for Isis and Nephthys. If anybody had enough energy, Sekhmet was taken for a run. Otherwise the three women took it in turn to throw sticks and a ball for her in the garden. She was not housed in the stables, but had a large kennel constructed out of an ancient garden shed which was in the grounds when Dr Rant bought the property.

As for Crozier Lodge itself, it had always been too large for the family's requirements, even while Dr Rant and his wife were alive, but his young partner had 'lived in' and occupied two of the rooms. Now that the sisters owned the house it was

more or less of a white elephant to them, even though a bedroom was always available for Susan if she were ever to elect to
stay overnight to assist with a whelping or to cope with any
other emergency.

Known locally merely as the Lodge, the house had eight
bedrooms, two bathrooms, drawing-room, dining-room, a
former library which had been converted into two consulting-
rooms, a morning-room which the two doctors had used as a
waiting-room for patients who attended morning and evening
surgery, and a large kitchen, a scullery and a butler's pantry.
Where the money came from to purchase such a property
formed a topic for discussion in the village, for Dr Rant was not
loved and had moved to Abbots Crozier from the Midlands, so
that he was received (and distrusted) as a foreigner. There was
even some dark speculation as to why he had ever left the
Midlands and a theory was bruited abroad that he had diddled
an elderly patient out of her money and had fled to escape
some embarrassing enquiries.

Apart from the garden shed which Sekhmet occupied, and
the stables which were now devoted to the six Pharaoh
hounds, there was one other outbuilding on the estate. The
ground floor of this was used as a garage, but there was an
outside stair to a room in which Dr Rant had stored junk and to
which the sisters, after their father's death, had added his
effects. The garage was kept locked when the car was inside,
but there was no lock on the door of the room above, although
it was at the top of an outside stair. In Bryony's opinion, there
was nothing in it worth stealing, and if a tramp chose to doss
down in it, well, it was a long way from the house.

Dr Rant's unpopularity had been added to by the deaths of
two patients through what the village regarded as gross careless-
ness if nothing worse. One of the deaths had been followed by
an inquest, for Dr Rant had refused to sign a death certificate
when certain rumours had come to his notice.

To add to the discontent, any medicines which might be
required had to be obtained from the chemist in Abbots Bay,

for there was no chemist's shop at that time in Abbots Crozier.
The villagers resented the long trudge downhill and up again
by the zigzag cliff path and still more the expenditure on the
cliff railway by those who were too infirm to do the stiff climb
back.

As one old man recollected, Dr Rant's predecessor had done
his own dispensing. When you went to the surgery you expected
to come away with a large bottle of pink medicine guaranteed to
cure all the ills that the flesh is heir to. Dr Rant, therefore,
started off on the wrong foot by requiring patients to present an
indecipherable prescription to a sea-board chemist whom they
believed could not read it any better than they could.

When Dr Rant died, his partner moved out and took a
house at Abbots Bay, so Abbots Crozier then had no doctor.

At nine on the evening of Goodfellow's visit, Bryony rang the
Stone House and apologised for bringing him over without
warning.

'I hope we shall never see him again,' she said to Dame
Beatrice. 'I am inclined to go to the Headlands hotel and find
out how long he is staying there. We don't want him badgering us again.'

'I think it would be inadvisable to go to his hotel. Your
motives would be misunderstood. You have done what you
could for him. I would leave it at that, if I were you. You can
always appeal to the police against a nuisance. There is just one
thing I would like to know. Did he give any indication of
knowing, before you brought him along, that you and your
sister were acquainted with me?'

'None at all. He said he needed a doctor to examine his knee
and then he went off into incoherent talk and a lot of silly
posturing. He alarmed us very much. We were desperate to
know what to do with him.'

'Did he make any mention of your Pharaoh hounds?'

'Yes, that was when he said he was Ozymandias, king of
kings. I suppose the word Pharaoh made some connection in

his mind. It was then that we decided he was mad. Morpeth went so far as to bring Osiris into the house, although not into the room where I was talking with Mr Goodfellow. She wanted to assure herself and him, Goodfellow, that we had some protection at hand.'

'I see. Well, I should dismiss him from your mind unless he pesters you. If he does, tell the police.'

'What worries me is that he had only to ask at the hotel if he really thought he needed a doctor. They would have referred him to Dr Mortlake down at Abbots Bay. Everybody goes to him now that my father is no more. As for the knee – well, there couldn't have been anything wrong with it. The Headlands is nearly halfway down the cliff and it's a very rough walk and all steeply uphill to get to us from there. Then, when he got here, he pirouetted about like a dancer. I'm sure he hadn't injured his knee. Well, I rang up only to apologise to you and to thank you for seeing him.'

'I don't think either thanks or an apology is due from you. We were interested to meet him, although I do not think we shall see him again.'

'Did he pay for the consultation?'

'No, but the interview hardly amounted to a consultation. He gave us an interesting interlude in our trivial round and I am grateful for that.'

About three-quarters of an hour later the telephone rang again at the Stone House and Laura answered it.

'That was Morpeth,' she said, when she returned to the room in which she had left Dame Beatrice.

'Don't tell me that she or her sister has disregarded my advice and gone to the Headlands hotel to check up on the length of Mr Goodfellow's stay there.'

'Not gone to it, but Bryony has rung it up. There is not, and never has been, a Mr Robin or any other Goodfellow staying there.'

'Interesting, but not surprising. He refused to name the hotel to us.'

*　　　*　　　*

The next bit of news also came from Crozier Lodge by telephone. Immediately after breakfast on the following day,
Bryony rang up to say, 'We have lost Sekhmet. We think she
has been stolen by a man who had put aniseed on his clothing.
Her kennel stinks of it. Susan went a while ago to look at
Sekhmet and found her gone. We've been all over the
grounds, but there's no sign of her. The strange thing is that
none of the hounds gave any warning that a thief was about.
Of course, Sekhmet's shed is a good way from the stables
where the hounds were, so, if he was very quiet and Sekhmet
herself didn't make any fuss, they may not have bothered, but
it seems strange. Their hearing is acute and, although they are
amenable creatures, I don't think they would tolerate an intruder about the place, particularly at night or before we were
up and about.'

'What are you going to do about it?'

'Susan is out now, with a couple of the hounds, looking for
her.'

'Is Sekhmet a valuable dog?'

'Well, not compared with the Pharaohs, so far as we are
concerned. That is our real worry. We wonder whether this was
a try-on to find out how easy it was to get into the grounds and
walk off with a dog. Of course, Sekhmet herself is an amiable
lunatic. She probably went off like a lamb and kept her nose
glued to the man's knee to drink in the lovely stink of the
aniseed.'

'Would it be as simple to steal a hound?'

'Gracious, no. The stable yard is locked when the hounds
are in at night and there is a high perimeter fence to enclose it
which nobody could climb and, anyway, the hounds would
gang up on him if anybody did get in.'

'Could not the dog have roamed off on her own?'

'We don't see how. There is no padlock on the front gates,
but Susan always shuts them after herself when she goes home
at night. For once, she went to look at Sekhmet even before she
came up to the house for breakfast, so we had early warning

that the dog was gone.'

'Is there a record of any other dogs having been stolen in your neighbourhood recently?'

'Not so far as we know, but not much of the local news comes our way. In any case, I shouldn't think the village dogs would be worth stealing. There is an Alsatian at the pub and the village poacher owns a lurcher, but I can't imagine either of them being much of a temptation to anybody, still less that they would go off with a stranger. Sekhmet, of course, is such a trusting fool that she would go off with anybody who spoke kindly to her.'

'So it was Susan, not one of yourselves, who discovered that Sekhmet had disappeared, was it?'

'Yes. At this time of year she comes along not later than half-past six. She went to the shed, found it empty, looked all about and then reported to us and we all searched and called, but when Susan mentioned the smell of aniseed we thought we knew what had happened, although we couldn't smell it in the shed.'

When the telephone call was over, Laura said to Dame Beatrice that it was strange that Susan had gone straight to Sekhmet's shed before breakfast. Dame Beatrice agreed, but added a rider to the effect that people did do strange things and that there was nobody more unpredictable than a more-or-less educated middle-aged spinster.

'We don't know that Susan is middle-aged,' said Laura. 'Anyway, a former theory comes back to me. Couldn't there be a connection between this dog-stealer, if there is one, and the mysterious prowler we've heard about? He taps on windows, apparently, and the Rants are too scared to go out and challenge him. Couldn't he have been making sure that the coast would be clear for dog-stealing because the Rants would never venture out of the house at night? It seems like that to me. Anyway, I'll give the Rants a ring after tea and ask whether Susan found Sekhmet.'

4

Dead in the River

When Laura made her telephone call, she was told an interesting story which was likely to last the village gossips and the frequenters of the only public house in Abbots Crozier for some time to come.

Susan's narrative had begun, as narratives should, at the beginning and it lost nothing in the telling or in Morpeth's version of it which came over the telephone.

That morning, Susan had tramped uphill by the zigzag path from Abbots Bay as usual and had found the hounds very restless. She had inspected each one and Nephthys, in particular, had seemed very unhappy. Susan let her and Isis out and although Isis only sniffed around as though she had detected some unusual aroma in the air, Nephthys made a bee-line for the garden shed.

Susan followed, for she had never known the bitch to do such a thing before. It was immediately clear that Sekhmet had gone. Susan called her by her 'calling' name – each dog had one, since their official names were not altogether suitable by which to summon them in public. Sekhmet was called Fret. Usually she came at once and made wild demonstrations of affection even to Susan, who had no use for them, but on this occasion she did not respond to her name.

Susan had been told about the prowler. She jumped to the conclusion that he had taken Sekhmet in mistake for a hound bitch – 'although he can't know much about dogs,' she said, 'if he couldn't tell a Labrador from a Pharaoh, even at night, when the job must have been done.'

She took Isis and Nephthys back to the stables, shut them away and let the other hounds out into the stable yard, then she went to the front gates. They had been shut, but, as usual, not locked when she arrived. When she had heard about the prowler she had suggested a chain and padlock, but, so far, this had not materialised, for the sisters were dilatory even though they were scared.

Susan reported up at the house, had a quick breakfast, leaving the sisters to finish theirs, and volunteered to go in search of the missing animal. She took Anubis and Amon with her, remarking before she left that if one of the dogs had to be enticed away 'poor old Sekhmet was most easily to be spared'. She loosed her two hounds into Sekhmet's shed, then put them in leash and sallied forth, hoping that they would be able to follow the aniseed scent.

She had had a hunch (she told the sisters on her return) that the thief would make for Abbots Bay. From there the main road led to Axehead, where there was a railway station, but if the man had a car, he could have taken the hill road to Abbots Crozier or left the car below on the sea front. The options were open.

Amon and Anubis ignored the entrance to the zigzag path and at first Susan thought that the smell of aniseed must have vanished in the keen morning air, and that the hounds, having nothing to guide them, were now intent on their accustomed run on the moor and were heading for their usual playground.

This did not prove to be the case. They rejected the right-hand turning with which they were familiar and proved that they had their minds on the job after all – for, when they had led her across a bridge and had reached a wicket gate which, to Susan's certain knowledge, they had never seen opened, they stopped, looked up at her and whined impatiently.

'Good boys,' she said. She opened the little gate and went with them on to a path beside the river. It led to one of the beauty spots of the neighbourhood and was a favourite walk for summer visitors.

As it happened – perhaps because it was still early morning – she met nobody. She released the hounds and they took her through a wooded glade on an uphill track, which, in spite of the summer weather, was still miry underfoot in places. She followed the river, less boisterous here than it would be when it reached the top of the cliffs and cascaded noisily down to Abbots Bay, and followed the hounds, who were obviously eager in pursuit of their quarry.

The rough path mounted and dipped and then mounted again until it reached the confluence of two streams at a very picturesque viewpoint known as Watersmeet. It looked no less beautiful, presumably, than usual, but more interesting.

Wedged in a cleft of the rocks over which the foaming waters were pouring lay the body of a man. His head was face-down under water and he was wearing nothing but a T-shirt and briefs. On the bank was a badly ripped pair of grey flannel trousers – and Sekhmet, sitting on them.

'Well, I'm damned!' said Susan to the hound. 'What the bloody hell have *you* been up to?' She did not touch Sekhmet, but waded into the swirling water. There was no doubt, however, that the man was dead, so she scrambled back again, gave Sekhmet a kick on the hind-quarters and said, 'Up!'

Sekhmet responded dutifully, but picked up the trousers in her powerful jaws and backed away with them.

'Oh, suit yourself,' said Susan. 'Home!' The two hounds cast around for a bit, but soon followed the woman and the Labrador. Sekhmet stumbled over the dragging trousers, but would not abandon them. Arrived back at Crozier Lodge, Susan returned the three dogs to their quarters and the last she saw of Sekhmet was a seemingly smiling and gratified animal once again seated on the trousers.

'So you found her,' said Bryony, when Susan went up to the house.

'Sure I found her. Mind if I use the phone? I found a drowned man, too. I think she took a chunk out of his trousers. He must have pulled them off and thrown them to her and then rushed into the river to get away from her. If he were still alive, I think it would be the last time he went in for dog-stealing. She brought the trousers home with her as battle honours, and if any policeman thinks he can take them away from her at present, he is welcome to try, but it would be as a *memento mori*, I fancy.'

'If she savaged this man,' said Morpeth, 'I suppose she will have to be put down.'

'Hold your horses!' said Susan. 'Let's find out first what the police have to say. I don't believe that silly old Fret would savage anybody. She wanted the trousers, that's all. I think that, when the man dashed into the river to get away from her, he missed his footing – those boulders must be as slippery as hell – fell over and bashed his head.' She went to the telephone and rang up the police at Axehead.

An inspector and a sergeant, both in uniform, appeared in due course and Susan conducted them to the confluence of waters where the dead man lay. They had come prepared and were wearing fishermen's waders. They slithered on the wet boulders, but retained their footing and soon had the dead man on the bank. There was a nasty disfiguring gash down one side of his face and the inspector was inclined to accept Susan's theory that the man had dashed into the river to escape the attentions of the dog and had slipped and fallen.

The sergeant had made an attempt to take the trousers away from Sekhmet, but she had turned so menacing and had guarded them so jealously that the inspector said, 'Leave her be. No sense in getting our fingers bitten off. Perhaps, miss,' (turning to Susan, who had been watching the manoeuvres with an indulgent and satirical smile) 'you could help.'

'Me?' said the kennel-maid. 'I can't spare *my* fingers, either. She can still smell the aniseed on the trousers, I expect. Once that wears off, I can get them for you easily enough if you really want them.'

'They will need to be inspected before the inquest, miss.'

'All right. I'll let you have them as soon as I can. It's suicide to try to take them away from her while she's in this mood.' So the police took away the body, having ascertained that the dead man was a complete stranger to the Rant sisters – though the sisters told them about the prowler. Later in the day, Morpeth had found Sekhmet lying out in the sunshine and had taken the opportunity to remove the trousers from the shed and take them indoors.

Here what turned out to be a significant discovery was made. A neat operation on the band of the trousers had completely removed the maker's name.

'Well, Sekhmet can't have done that,' said Morpeth. 'That has been done with a sharp pair of scissors, not torn out by an enthusiastic dog.'

'But why?' asked her sister.

'To disguise ownership, of course. I think he was our prowler.'

'But he had no reason to think that we should ever have seen inside the waistband of his trousers. Where is Susan?'

'Out with Isis and Nephthys, as usual.'

'Oh, yes, of course. Well, Amon and Anubis had their run this morning and all the excitement of tracking Sekhmet and finding the body, so that lets you out for today if you like, although I must take out my two. You might let the police know that we've got the trousers, although I can't see why they should be needed at the inquest. Give Susan her tea directly she comes in and a meat pasty to take home for her supper. I'm surprised she was willing to go out again. She must have had a nasty shock when she found the dead man, so she may be very glad to get home early and turn in. Give her a bottle of the elderberry wine. She deserves it.'

Morpeth showed Susan the trousers when the kennel-maid came in. Susan examined the hole in the waistband and said, 'I don't want to put ideas into your head, but what do you think of the hole?'

'What do you mean, Susan?' asked Morpeth anxiously.

'I think, for Sekhmet's sake, the police will have to look at these trousers,' replied Susan. 'No dog made that hole. A piece has been cut clean out of the garment with a pair of sharp scissors.'

'Well,' said Morpeth, 'I can tell you this: there were no scissors in the pockets when I picked the trousers up and took them from the kennel after Sekhmet lost interest in them. There was nothing in the pockets at all. As for Sekhmet, she's probably got her nose against the wires of the stable-yard enclosure by now and is trying to attract the attention of Osiris or one of the others. She was lying asleep in the garden when I took the trousers. There was nothing else near her or in her den. That man seems to have been determined to hide his identity, but, then, if he was our prowler –'

'I don't like the look of it,' said Bryony, when she came home after Susan had gone off with the wine and her supper. 'If he had no scissors or sharp knife, somebody else could have cut his trousers, although for what purpose I can't begin to think, unless the death was not accidental. It's a pity there was nothing in the pockets. The police love fingerprints and diaries and old letters with indecipherable postmarks.'

'Well,' said Laura to Dame Beatrice, after finishing her telephone conversation with Morpeth, 'do we brave the same fate as Jezebel?'

'Oh, what did the Rant sisters have to say?'

'It appears that the ill-advised dog-thief who drenched his trousers in aniseed has now lost not only the trousers but his life. He got a nasty knock on the head and Susan, the gifted kennel-maid, tracked down him and the bitch he had walked off with and found the body.'

'Why have we been summoned? Your remark concerning Queen Jezebel indicates that we are invited to call at Crozier Lodge and be eaten by dogs.'

'It's a *Mayday Mayday* cry of distress. They don't like the look of things and are asking for expert advice. I said I would ring back when I had spoken to you.'

'What aspect of the matter has alarmed them?'

'Morpeth said she would tell us the whole story if we would go over there. Do you feel inclined to brave these Hounds of the Baskervilles some time tomorrow?'

'We must not be found wanting in womanly sympathy. I suppose they have notified the police?'

'Oh, yes. That's what's worrying them.'

'Well, one hardly likes to suppose that Susan hit the man over the head and stole his trousers. She has trousers of her own.'

'I suppose you do intend to go and see the Rants?' said Laura, ignoring this piece of persiflage.

'Nothing would keep me away. The sisters are interesting persons, Susan is a somewhat mysterious figure. The hounds, I trust, will be under restraint when we arrive and I cannot wait to hear the whole story – if possible, from Susan herself.'

This was told them when they arrived after lunch the following day at Crozier Lodge. The dog hounds were in their stables compound, Isis and Nephthys were occupying two armchairs in the study with the door closed on them, and Sekhmet, who appeared to think that she was in bad odour, had accompanied Susan to the main gates when the visitors rang the bell. She gave every indication of wanting to ingratiate herself with them, but refused to accompany them up to the front door.

'I think she's saying she's sorry she stole the trousers,' said Susan, 'but it's a bit late for that now. Bryony and Morpeth think she may have landed us in for trouble, but I don't see how that can be. Oh, well, I'll leave you with them. They know everything that I know.'

'That will not do,' said Dame Beatrice firmly. 'We have had their version and have been called into consultation. What we need now is a first-hand account from a primary source. The police will not allow matters to rest where they are. Speak freely and at whatever length you like.'

'Leaving out no detail, however slight,' said Laura. 'Your story will be of the utmost interest.'

Susan repeated the account she had given the sisters. The listeners heard her without interrupting the narrative and then Dame Beatrice asked, 'Would Sekhmet have turned savage in her desire to obtain possession of the trousers?'

'Never known her to go nasty on anybody,' said Morpeth.

'But, then,' put in Bryony, 'I don't think she has had much opportunity to show her seamy side, if she's got one. Nobody ever comes across the garden. The tradespeople won't approach the house. We have to go along and take in the post and the goods, or whatever, when the bell rings. We are not exactly popular in the village.'

'The man must have been in a panic to have abandoned his trousers,' remarked Dame Beatrice.

'What on earth would the police have to say if he walked into the next village in his underpants?' said Laura.

'I shall never believe Sekhmet scared him so much that he let her have his trousers,' said Morpeth. 'Actually, she's affectionate to the point of being a nuisance, but she would never frighten anybody.'

'The fact remains that he did part with the trousers and he even seems to have dashed into the river to get away from her,' said Laura.

'That does appear to have been an unnecessary proceeding,' said Dame Beatrice, 'if the trousers were all the dog wanted. Were they dry or wet when you found Sekhmet sitting on them?'

'Dry, except where she'd slobbered over them,' replied Susan. 'He would hardly have taken them off in the river, especially as he had slipped and bashed his head.'

'Can you prove at what time you left Abbots Bay to walk up here yesterday morning?'

'Not unless somebody saw me leave my cottage,' said Susan, surprised and somewhat disconcerted by the question. 'I walked up from Abbots Bay – I usually do, because the cliff railway doesn't function so early in the morning – and I don't remember meeting a soul. I saw nobody on the path to

Watersmeet, either. I suppose I shall have to give evidence at the inquest.'

'Of course,' said Dame Beatrice. 'You cannot say for certain that the trousers the dog was guarding are the trousers which belonged to the dead man. You never saw him wearing them.'

Susan looked surprised and disconcerted again.

'They must have been his,' she said. 'He wasn't wearing trousers when I saw him in the river.'

'Which proves nothing. What was to prevent an attacker giving the hound another pair of trousers sprinkled with aniseed to keep her occupied while he removed the garment from his victim's dead body, and made off with whatever was in the pockets?'

'Oh, but, surely that is a fantastic suggestion!' exclaimed Morpeth.

'I merely throw it out as such,' said Dame Beatrice. 'Did you find the square of cloth which had been so neatly cut out of the trousers?' she added, turning to Susan.

'No, I didn't.'

'Would Sekhmet have gone into the stream after the man?'

'No. For one thing, the sound of the rushing water would have put her off, I'm sure. In any case, she was quite dry when I found her.'

'Well, we must see what the police think of it all,' said Dame Beatrice. 'You will have to answer a good many questions, I am afraid.'

'You'll stand by us, won't you?' said Morpeth.

The inquest, held in the parish hall, was sparsely attended, for it happened on a Tuesday and began at ten in the morning when the villagers were out at work or busy in the house or looking after summer-holiday guests. In any case, not much interest was taken in a drowning fatality. Such deaths were far from unknown to the twin villages. The coast was inhospitable and dangerous and the river, in a never-to-be-forgotten spate in the year 1952, had shown what it could do in the way of danger to life and the destruction of property.

There would have been more interest shown had the man been a native of the place, but in this case the dead was a stranger and, to that extent, expendable. In fact, the first difficulty the coroner encountered was that, so far, the corpse remained unidentified. Nobody had come forward to say who he was or where he came from. Though his face had been badly disfigured, a rough artist's impression had been posted up outside the police station. There had been appeals in the local press and the police had made patient house-to-house and hotel-to-hotel enquiries, but without result. An enterprising young reporter had even suggested to his editor that the Kennel Club should be approached with a request for the names and addresses of the known breeders of Pharaoh hounds, but this suggestion had been turned down.

'We could land ourselves in trouble,' said the editor, 'if it seemed we were implying that one of these breeders employs a dog-stealer, and that's what your half-baked notion amounts to, my boy.'

The police had not been able to find the square of cloth which had been cut from the trousers, but the medical evidence was clear as to the cause of death. The man had not been savaged by the dog. He had died from concussion followed by drowning. There were no marks of a dog's teeth on the body, and when the trousers were produced it was clear that these had not been attacked by Sekhmet, either, as no dog could have effected so neat a hole in the material.

Susan was called upon to testify to her discovery of the body. She went on to assure the court (and was backed up firmly but unofficially by Bryony from the public benches) that Sekhmet had never attempted to attack anybody, but had been fascinated by the smell of the aniseed which had been sprinkled lavishly on the trousers.

The vet from Axehead testified that he was called occasionally to Crozier Lodge to inoculate puppies against the various diseases to which puppies are liable and, later, to give the necessary 'boosters'. The adult dogs, he said, were amenable and without vice, good guard dogs, but trustworthy, well cared for and well trained.

The police sergeant agreed. He had been present with the inspector and had seen the body in the river. There had never been any complaints about the behaviour of the Crozier Lodge hounds. He had a dog of his own and knew that dog-stealers often sprayed aniseed on their trousers. Dogs would follow the scent of it anywhere.

'Let us look,' said the sergeant – a young man who was well read, 'at *The Episode of the Dog McIntosh*.'

'The dog did *what*?'

'No, sir. McIntosh was the name of the dog in question.'

'That is not the name given me by the last witness.'

'I refer, sir, to the dog in the *Episode*.'

'Oh, I see. A scottie, I suppose.'

'An Aberdeen terrier, sir, yes.'

'Prefer West Highland myself,' commented the coroner, 'but what has that dog to do with this present enquiry?'

'I advanced it as an instance of the effect the smell of aniseed has on the canine population. The *Episode* concerns the abstraction of the dog McIntosh from a London apartment (to which it should not have been taken) by means of this same device, sir.'

'What same device?'

'The device of sprinkling aniseed on the trousers, sir.'

'Oh, we've got to the point at last, have we? Has it ever occurred to you, sergeant, that you are wasted in the police force and would stand an excellent chance of getting into Parliament and wasting the time of the House instead of *my* time?'

(In parenthesis it may be revealed that the well-read sergeant did leave the Force. He took a course in teacher training, became a schoolmaster and later the head of a school. In the course of time he also was appointed to serve on the local Bench, where he was the terror of young constables who were called upon to give evidence. It was his habit to warn them: 'Now, be very careful, officer. I have been a member of the police force myself and know all the dodges.')

The medical examination had concluded that, although the head wound had not been fatal in itself, it had been the contributory factor in the subsequent drowning. There was nothing to show whether a piece had been cut from the trousers at the scene of the accident or previously, so there was no proof that another person had been present before Susan saw the body.

The inference that the man, embarrassed by the attentions of Sekhmet, had abandoned his trousers to her and had leapt into the river to get away from her, still stood, ridiculous though it sounded. The verdict was that, in doing so, he had slipped on the treacherous boulders, knocked himself unconscious and had subsequently drowned as the result of this accident.

5

Theories and Speculations

'So we suspect that there has been dirty work at the crossroads or, in this case, at the confluence of the waters,' said Laura, when she and Dame Beatrice were back at the Stone House. 'What are you going to do about it? According to the verdict we heard pronounced, the answer is a lemon.'

'There are various ways of dealing with dirty work,' said Dame Beatrice.

'Name two.'

'Well, there is the way adopted by the priest and the Levite in the story of the good Samaritan – pass by on the other side of the road and so avoid all chance of becoming implicated. Another way is to proceed with some dirty work of one's own. I fail to see how lemons come into the matter.'

'Just a manner of saying that the verdict has shut all doors to further investigation of that de-trousered fellow's death.'

'Not necessarily. The circumstances are bizarre and therefore, to that extent, interesting. Further interest is added by the fact that Bryony shares our suspicions.'

'It's a pity Sekhmet can't talk.'

'I hardly think Susan would agree with you.'

'Do you think the dead man was the Crozier Lodge prowler?'

'Time will tell, perhaps.'

'It seems a bit much to suspect Susan on no evidence at all.'

'We have only Susan's word for it that the man was dead when she got to Watersmeet. Her wet jeans could be (and no doubt were) explained by her statement that she waded into the river to look at the body. She is the one person, apart from the two sisters, who could be quite sure that Sekhmet would not attack her, whatever she did.'

'The evidence is that Sekhmet would not attack anybody.'

'I am acting as the Devil's advocate, as usual, but one must always be prepared to look at a problem from all sides.'

'You don't deny that somebody enticed Sekhmet away with intent to steal her, do you?'

'I have an open mind about the question of stealing her. Why steal a comparatively valueless Labrador bitch when there are two pedigree Pharaoh hounds of the same sex at Crozier Lodge? It does not strike me as a very sensible procedure.'

'Oh, well, yes, there is that, I suppose. The smell of aniseed would have attracted the other hounds as much as it did Sekhmet, but, of course, the answer is that all the Pharaohs were shut safely away, so Sekhmet was the only dog available.'

'We come now to the question of the mutilated trousers.'

'Well, if the circumstances of the death were more suspicious than the inquest verdict would have us believe, there is no doubt why that particular chunk was chopped out of them, although there is no reason to think Susan did that. It would have shown the name of the tailor or outfitter who had supplied the pants and the police are pretty hot at tracing people when they've got that much to go on. On the other hand, if the death was purely accidental, surely somebody will turn up at some time and report this man as missing.'

'A question which ought to have been raised at the inquest is whether the trousers on which Sekhmet was sitting were the trousers of the dead man or of somebody else. They could be the murderer's own trousers (if murder has been committed) and he could have gone off in the victim's garments.'

'Well, that would let Susan out, surely?'

'Who can tell? The Rant sisters could say what she was wearing when she went off to Watersmeet, no doubt, but –'

'I think you are trailing your coat. What do you expect me to do about it?'

'Tread on the tail of it, of course, and challenge every suggestion I make. The more we argue, the more likely we are to arrive at some aspect of the truth.'

'You really do believe this is a case of murder, don't you?'

'*Believe* is too definite a word. I certainly think there are strong reasons for keeping the possibility of foul play in the forefront of our minds. Presumably the man and the hound had been in amicable relationship on their walk, so it seems strange that he panicked at Watersmeet, discarded his trousers – surely not easy if the dog was paying him the close attention which has been postulated – and then that, having bestowed the garments on her, he leapt into the torrent. The whole suggestion seems to me bizarre in the extreme.'

'But so is your own suggestion that the murderer hit the man over the head, changed into the man's trousers and then wedged the body among the boulders in the river.'

'*Touché!*' said Dame Beatrice, leering at her secretary. 'Both theories are idiotic. We must return to the subject later.'

'No, honestly, tell me what you *really* think happened.'

'My thoughts do not appear to impress you.'

'Well, you've admitted that they do seem a bit far-fetched. Don't you think the verdict of accidental death may be the right one after all?'

'I might, were it not that possible evidence of identity had been cut out of the trousers. I do not see how the significance of *that* can be overlooked.'

'The coroner and the police seem to have overlooked it.'

'They may have thought that the trousers had been made to fit more comfortably when the piece of the waistband was removed. I daresay that if you asked the opinion of that erudite young detective-sergeant, he would quote you the case of *The Aunt and the Sluggard*.'

'To what purpose?'

'I seem to remember that, when Rockmetteller Todd borrowed Bertram Wooster's dress clothes, he split the waistcoat up the back in order to make it more comfortable to wear.'

'You think of everything,' said Laura, in mock admiration.

'All the same, having made my point, I will now retract. I do not believe that anybody had chopped a piece out of the waistband of those trousers for the purpose of making them more comfortable to wear. I do think there has been murder committed and I am sufficiently interested to pursue the matter further, although I shall not assume Susan's guilt unless or until I can find proof of it.'

'Well, thank goodness *that's* all over,' said Bryony. She glanced at the clock. 'Isn't it time you took Amon and Anubis out for their run?'

'Can't we shut Isis and Nephthys and Sekhmet in the house and give my two the run of the garden just for once?'

'Why?'

'I don't feel like going out.'

'Not feeling seedy, are you?'

'No, just disinclined to leave the house, that's all.'

'Suit yourself. It's no good letting this wretched drowning get you down, though, you know. If that man had not tried to steal poor old Fret, he would still be alive, no doubt.'

'I know. I just don't fancy going out, that's all.'

'You ought to watch yourself, Morpeth.' Bryony looked at her sister with sympathy mixed with slight exasperation and a certain amount of anxiety. 'Once you start this kind of opting out, you may find it grows on you. You don't want to end up with agoraphobia.'

'You always fly to extremes when you criticise me. The fact is, I can't get that strange Ozymandias man out of my head. I don't intend to get mixed up with him again, and somehow I can't help connecting him with this drowning.'

'Absolute nonsense!'

'Suppose he were to pop out on me when I was out with the dogs and begin gibbering at me! I should be shattered with terror.'

'Good gracious! The hounds would chew him up if he threatened you.'

'There might be other conclusions about Sekhmet if any of the hounds savaged Ozymandias.'

'Oh, forget about that lunatic. Look here, I'll take Amon and Anubis for their run, if you like. I shan't be all that long. That inquest ate into the morning. Put lunch back a bit, will you? I'll be back at half one.'

Morpeth accompanied her to the door. They found Sekhmet with her nose against it. As it was opened, she shot past the pair of them and made for the drawing-room. Bryony followed, ousted her unceremoniously from an armchair and said, 'No!' The bitch looked at her meltingly, but Bryony hustled her off the chair and conducted her into the garden.

'A fine mess you seem to have got us into,' she said to the dog severely, 'you and your damned aniseed.'

Sekhmet dropped her tail dejectedly as Bryony conducted her to her kennel. When she rejoined Morpeth, Bryony said, 'There never was any smell of aniseed in that shed so far as I could ever detect.'

'I suppose it's very volatile,' said Morpeth. 'I'll come with you as far as the gate.'

'I don't know what has come over you, Morpeth. You've taken your hounds out every day since Susan found the body. Why suddenly change like this?'

'I don't know. The inquest has upset me.'

On the way through the wilderness they called the garden, they met Susan.

'Hullo,' she said, noting Bryony's wellingtons and Morpeth's sneakers. 'What's afoot, then? Swopping partners or something?'

'Bryony is going out today instead of me.'

'Oh, why is that? Aren't you well?'

Morpeth gave her the reason she had given Bryony. 'The inquest upset me, I think.'

'Well, I must say the influence it had on me was to buck me

up. No accounting for reflexes and reactions. The verdict completely exonerated old Fret. She looks a bit dejected. Come on, Fret! Raise your flag!'

Bryony left her with the bitch and she and Morpeth collected the two hounds; Bryony passed out of the grounds with them and headed for the moor. Curiosity, however, and some other impulse which she could not define, caused Bryony to diverge from the usual track and take a path which led to the bridge over the river and the wicket-gate which opened up the way to Watersmeet. Here she slipped the leads.

Nothing loth, the hounds poured themselves through the aperture and were soon enjoying themselves among the trees and bushes. Bryony kept to the path alongside the water and looked at the river, silver in the light, flecked with foam on the wilder reaches and dappled under the banks by the sunshine glinting through the trees.

It was about a mile and a half to Watersmeet. Here she stopped and gazed at the confluence of the two streams. The rapids lacked the depth and grandeur of Aysgarth Force, the beauty of the Falls of Rogie or the cascading hill-top tumble and roar of Ardessie, all of which Bryony had seen, but, although they were on a smaller scale, the rapids at Watersmeet were reminiscent, because of their woodland surroundings and the way they foamed over the boulders, of the Falls of Bracklinn, she thought.

They were also not unlike the Falls of Dochart, either, Bryony decided, remembering holiday photographs she had taken when she and her sister had gone with their father on holiday to Scotland, although the scene at Watersmeet certainly lacked the backdrop of the mountains behind Killin.

She stood there for some time and then whistled up the hounds, intending to walk on for about half a mile to where a rustic bridge led across the upper waters to a hotel where she could get a drink at the bar. Amon came at her call, but Anubis did not appear.

'Find!' commanded Bryony of the obedient hound. 'Find

Nubi!' She went with the dog, calling the other's pet name;
still Anubis did not appear. The other hound, however, knew
where he was, for he led Bryony beyond the belt of trees and
bushes, and there was Anubis with his nose to a hole in the
bank of soft earth.

'If you think I've brought you out to go rabbiting, you've
got another think coming. Anyway, that isn't a rabbit hole,
fathead!' Bryony put a lead on the dog's collar and hauled him
away. Beyond the trees the bank was in full sunshine. Bryony
looped the lead over a bush and wondered what Anubis had
found. She rolled up her sleeve and reached into the hole. In it
she unearthed a sharp, heavy piece of stone. The pointed end
of it was stained as though with rust. Bryony, whose fingers
could reach where the dog's muzzle could not go, had soon
prised the stone out of its resting place. She inspected it
closely. Then she spat on it and rubbed the damp little patch
with her handkerchief. The coagulated blood yielded a dirty
reddish stain.

'Oh, Lord!' said Bryony under her breath. 'That's torn the
verdict at the inquest, my God it has!' She carried the stone
over to the river, waded in (thankful that she was wearing
wellingtons) and dropped it into the water in midstream.
Then, as an extra precaution, she picked it up again and
pushed it point downwards between two large boulders before
she waded ashore.

She was only just in time. Voices could be heard and,
putting Amon also in leash, she strode off along the riverside
track towards the rustic bridge and the pub.

'You've been a long time. We're starving,' said Susan.

'Luckily it's only cold ham, new potatoes and peas,' said
Morpeth, 'and we can steam up the veg. Where on earth have
you been?'

'She got lost on the moor,' said Susan, 'or else she stopped
at the Whortleberry in Clapbridge and had a couple.'

'Well, as a matter of fact, I did just that. The bar was

crowded with holidaymakers, so it took ages for me to get served and then people were interested in the hounds and that delayed me. One has to be civil.'

'I thought they didn't have dogs in the bar at the Whortle-berry.'

'Oh, the hounds weren't taken inside. I carried my drinks to the only table out of doors where there was a vacant seat, and the other people there made a terrific fuss of the dogs and fed them snacks. I don't know how I ever got them away. They drooled and dribbled and made friends with everybody.'

'That was a change for them, then,' said Susan sceptically. 'They don't usually take any too quickly to strangers.'

'It was the food, of course. Chicken sandwiches, bits of liver sausage, cake, biscuits – you name it, they had it.'

'Then they'll probably keep us up all night. We'll be lucky if we don't have to call in the vet.'

'Oh, Susan! A bit of a treat now and again doesn't hurt them. We hardly spoil them here, do we? Besides, I am sure they digested it all on the long walk home,' said Morpeth.

'If you went across the moor as far as the Whortleberry, it certainly *was* a long walk home,' said Susan.

Her tone was dry and Morpeth looked at her in some per-plexity. Bryony, hoping that her flushed cheeks did not betray that she had been lying, seated herself at the dining-table and demanded to be fed. When Susan had gone home to her cottage in Abbots Bay after supper that night and the dishes had been cleared away and washed up, Morpeth said, 'What's up? What *really* happened while you were out this morning? You didn't really go to the Whortleberry, did you?'

'Well, no, but nothing happened, nothing at all.'

'You might as well tell me. I shan't give you any peace until you do. Anybody could see you were lying when you talked about the hounds and their sandwiches and things.'

But Bryony, as she began to explain, had not been lying about the sandwiches and other treats which the hounds had enjoyed. The only lie she had told was that these treats had not been given at the Whortleberry inn on the moor, but at the hotel beyond Watersmeet.

Morpeth was silent for a minute when this was made plain. Then she said, 'So you took Amon and Anubis to Watersmeet. Why? We never cake the hounds along the river. Too many summer visitors and boys throwing stones.'

Bryony found difficulty in explaining what had caused her to take the riverside path, since she knew that it had been her own curiosity, after she had heard the verdict at the inquest, which had given her the incentive to go and study the spot where the body had been found. She was torn between an urgent desire to share the news about the blood-stained stone and a fear that she had done a very wrong thing in trying to hide the evidence of what must have been a vicious attack on somebody. She had tried to convince herself that it was unlikely that the stone had had any connection with the death of the so-far unidentified victim, but there could be little doubt that somebody had pushed the stone into the hole in the bank. The only obvious reason for such an action could have been the intention to hide it.

It was not often that Morpeth was in command of any situation which arose between herself and her elder sister. She pressed home her advantage.

'Come on,' she said. 'We don't have secrets from one another. You went to Watersmeet, goodness knows why, and something happened there, didn't it?'

'Nothing happened, I tell you. Stop badgering me. Why shouldn't I go to Watersmeet? Of course I was interested in 'seeing the place.'

'It's days since Susan found that dead man. If you are morbid enough to visit the spot marked with an X, why have you waited until now?'

'I don't know why.'

'You didn't run into Ozymandias, did you?'

'No, of course not.'

'I was scared of him. He's quite definitely mad.'

'I didn't meet him, I tell you. I didn't meet anybody until I got to the hotel.'

'What *did* happen, then? Tell me.'

'I had better not. The fewer people who know, the better.'

'We have never kept secrets from one another. I've said so. Anyway, I was always better at keeping them than you were.'

'Because you're an introvert and I'm an extrovert, that's why. Introverts are always secretive. You shouldn't be proud of the fact.'

'Be that as it may, you know you can trust me.'

Because of her need to confide in somebody, Bryony gave in.

'Morpeth,' she said, 'I think I found the stone which killed that man Susan found in the river. At least, I myself didn't find it. One of the hounds did.'

'But where? You couldn't know that's what it was if you found it in the river.'

'I didn't find it in the river. I only put it there after I had winkled it out of a hole in the bank.'

'What bank?'

Having committed herself thus far, Bryony came out with the whole story. She concluded it by saying, 'Well, I hauled Anubis away from the hole and found this stone with the rusty stains. I didn't see how rust could get on to a stone, so I wetted it and rubbed it with my handkerchief. It came off a dirty red colour. Oh, Morpeth, I'm sure it was blood.'

'Well, you had better tell the police. They can make tests. It probably wasn't blood at all. We know the man had a head wound. You simply put two and two together. Anybody else would have done the same. Not to worry. If you planted the stone in the river, it's probably washed clean by this time. The river was tumbling down quite fast, I suppose. All the same, you may find it a bit embarrassing when you tell the police what you did. I can see why you feel troubled.'

'I have no intention of telling them anything. Neither must you.'

'But if you think that man was attacked –'

'Look, there are three reasons for keeping our mouths shut. First, I might be in dead trouble for destroying evidence of a crime. Second, the last thing we want is to upset the fortunate verdict at the inquest.'

'Fortunate?'

'Of course. Any moderately intelligent person would see that there was something distinctly odd, to say the least, about that piece of cloth being cut – *cut*, not torn – out of the trousers.'

'Oh, I don't know. People do the most extraordinary things to their clothes.'

'Third, and most important, we have to protect Susan.'

'Good gracious! You don't *really* think Susan attacked the man, do you? I know we did wonder, but when we were sure it was not Ozymandias –'

'But we're *not* sure. We never saw the body. Whoever it was, if Susan found him ill-treating Sekhmet after he stole her, or if he kicked one of the hounds she had taken with her, I would not go bail for anything Susan might do. Have you forgotten how she collared and thrashed the butcher's boy when he got Nephthys in the ribs with a half-brick? She's as strong as a horse and doesn't give a damn for anybody. I wouldn't put anything past her if she was in a rage.'

'She would never go so far as murder.'

'Intentionally, perhaps not, although I wouldn't take my oath on that either. She is capable of extreme violence. All the same, I don't forget that the doctors didn't say the head wound *killed* the man. Actually it was brought in as accidental death by drowning. I think it more than likely that the man annoyed Susan, that she attacked him with this sharp piece of stone, that she then attempted to hide it in this hole in the bank, that she then realised that he was unconscious, so de-trousered him and chucked the trousers to Fret to keep her occupied, and then dumped the man in the river, perhaps with the idea that the cold water would revive him.'

'Oh, Bryony, she couldn't have done! I'll never believe it. Besides, why would she chop a bit out of the trousers? She wouldn't have had any scissors, for one thing.'

'See here, Morpeth. The man is dead. Nothing can bring him back to life. We must let the matter rest. Do you really want to have another inquest and another verdict, and police and the press and crowds of morbid sightseers swarming all over the place?'

'No, of course I don't. All right, then, I'll keep absolutely quiet about what you've told me. All the same, innocent blood, you know, cries from the ground for vengeance. We are told so.'

'This wasn't innocent blood. He was attempting to steal one of our dogs.'

'Well, if you suspect Susan as you say you do –'

'Suspicion is not proof. I don't propose to accuse her of anything. I simply want things left exactly as they are and the verdict given at the inquest to stand. I don't want this business stirred up again.'

'All I was going to say is that, if you think as you do, we must get rid of Susan. We can't possibly keep her here.'

'And blow the lid off the whole thing? I refuse to think of Susan as a murderess, although she may have been an agent of death, as I believe she was. Anyway, we can't do without her. You know that, as well as I do. She manages the hounds far better than you and I can. Besides, I am going only on suspicion and surmise, and that is very wrong of me. There isn't an atom of proof against her. We must remember that.'

'But we may be shielding *another* murderer, not Susan at all.'

'We must take our chance of it, I'm afraid.'

6

The Poacher's Story

'I've got another of those nutters outside, sir,' said the desk sergeant to Police Inspector Burfield. 'Name of Adams.'

'Not somebody else who wants to tell us he knows who murdered that man we took out of the river?'

'That's right, sir. He's the fourth since Thursday. It's that poacher chap. Shouldn't have thought he was a nutcase. Out for what he can get, I reckon.'

'I'd better see him. Looks as though we're not the only people who thought the verdict given at the inquest was more than a bit doubtful. All right, send him in.'

The individual who was shown in was utterly unlike any of the three earlier visitors to whom the sergeant had referred. One of these had claimed to be clairvoyant; another was an escapee from a mental hospital who had been claimed by the authorities almost before he had concluded a confession that he was a murderer; the third had been a pseudo-clergyman, eccentric but harmless, who said that he had witnessed the murder in what he called a vision. As none of his description tallied even slightly with anything which the police knew, he had been dismissed, like the clairvoyant, with a promise that 'we will look into it'.

The present claimant to knowledge was a wiry, ferret-faced man wearing, in spite of the fine summer weather, a long overcoat which, to the police inspector's experienced eye, housed a poacher's pocket. He had seen Adams before. He said to the disreputable man, 'Well, what's *your* problem? Keep it short. I'm busy.'

'To come to the point, then, sir, I was wondering whether a bit of information might be worth a bob or two.'

'Information about what?'

'This bloke as was found in the river up about Abbots Crozier.'

Burfield did not betray the fact that he was interested. He said, 'That's all over and done with. We've held the inquest.'

'You mean you knows who he was?'

'No, we don't know who he was. The inquest decided that the death was the result of an accident.'

'And what if it wasn't? What if somebody bashed him over the napper?'

'You're wasting my time. You own a dog, don't you?'

'Sort of.'

'Licensed?'

''Course she's licensed. What do you take me for?'

'You wouldn't like it if I told you. What about those pheasants I heard about last autumn?'

'I don't never go trespassing after pheasants, sir. I only takes what I knows to be ferry naturee, such as rabbits and that.'

'Fairy what?'

'No, sir. Meaning as they don't belong of nobody, so is a free-for-all. That's all I ever takes, sir.'

'If you've anything useful to say, say it and be off. If you think you know who the dead man was, you had better tell me. It's a serious thing to withhold evidence.'

'I can't put a name to him, but I can tell you where he was dossing down the night before he was killed.'

The Axehead police had continued to make enquiries in their attempt to identify the dead man, but all efforts had proved to be in vain. Nobody appeared to have known him. The inspector jingled some silver in his pocket.

'All right. Come across with it,' he said. The story which emerged was circumstantial, but Burfield was inclined to think that it was true. Unfortunately it was of no immediate help in identifying the man found in the river.

According to the poacher, who lived in a shack on the moor about three miles from Crozier Lodge, on the morning in question he had gone at first light to look at some snares he had set and found that he had caught five rabbits. He had decided to offer them to the Rant sisters, as he often did – 'them dogs of theirs being partial to a bit of rabbit' – so he had taken them along to Crozier Lodge.

'All five?' asked Burfield.

'Yes, sir, being that I'd been up to the hills a day or two before and had a nice hare hanging up ready for my own pot, hares on the mountain being anybody's for the hunting, as the old song says.'

'That lurcher of yours will land you in trouble one of these days.'

Adams ignored this warning and went on with his tale. Thinking that it was a little early to disturb the ladies – it being, he reckoned, not much past five in the morning – and being unwilling to carry five plump rabbits to his shack and then transport them later in the day to Crozier Lodge, he did as he had done before on similar occasions. He went to the back door of Crozier Lodge, which he had always found unlocked, opened it and deposited the rabbits on the kitchen table. When his occasions took him that way again, he proposed to call for his money and get the two thick slices of home-made bread and good beef dripping which were his perks when he made such visits. There was never any difficulty in getting paid for the rabbits, he explained, the ladies being as honest as the day and not the sort to try to do a good man down.

What he did not know at the time, although Morpeth told him later, was that, since the sisters had learned that they had a night prowler, they always locked and bolted both the back and front doors, so, for the first time, he could not get in.

He did not want to knock anybody up, so he thought of leaving the rabbits in the garage, where he assumed they would soon be found, but the garage also had been made secure. He then mounted the outside stair to the garage loft.

Matters, however, did not turn out as he had hoped. The door to the upper room was not locked, so he had opened it and was about to step over the threshold into the very dimly lighted chamber when he heard somebody moving about. He supposed it was a tramp and – 'me being what you might call a bantam-weight, sir' – he had decided to make a discreet withdrawal rather than risk annoying the vagrant by invading his sleeping quarters.

'Oh, yes?' said Burfield. 'And, having read the papers, I suppose the minute you opened the door you detected a strong smell of aniseed.'

'Aniseed, sir? Why should I? Anyway, I didn't smell nothing unexpected beyond what you'd expect.'

'Never been in the dog-stealing business, then? Oh, never mind. Go on.'

In turning, Adams had caught his heel and dropped the rabbits – 'being as I'd tied up their back legs and put 'em along a stick as I carries so I can put the stick acrorst my shoulder with four of the rabbits hanging from it two by two and t'other un in my overcoat pocket'. Burfield said that he fancied he knew all about that pocket, but that the matter need not be discussed at this juncture.

The noise must have been heard by the tramp. He gave a shout and Adams could hear a chair, a decrepit object, but a favourite, perhaps, at one time, with Dr Rant, creaking as the occupant pushed it aside. Adams had retrieved the stick and the rabbits, flung himself down the stone stair and hidden himself away round by the side of the garage, hoping that the tramp would not try to find out the reason for the disturbance.

The next thing Adams heard was a curse and then the sound of the door at the top of the staircase being shut. He did not know at the moment whether the man up above him was now inside or outside the building, although he assumed that the curse was because the fellow had stumbled, as he himself had done. However, it was soon clear that somebody had emerged from the loft, for the next thing was the sound of footsteps on the stone staircase.

Adams remained where he was, hoping that the man, realising that somebody was about, would now take flight. He himself remained in hiding until he thought the coast would be clear, but he did lean out to get a glimpse of the man. Then he crept forward and could see the tramp walking rapidly across the garden towards the big gates. Thinking that the man would soon be gone, he went back into hiding in case the other looked round.

'I give him all of five minutes, I reckon, sir,' he said, 'but when I ventures forth I seen that, far from slinging his hook, as I had thought he would, blowed if he wasn't still halfway down the garden and off to the side by what was the old garden shed afore the ladies turned it into a kind of a kennel and, what's more, he was stood there a-talking to somebody.

'Of course I thought at first as it must be one of the ladies as had got up extra early to take one or two of the dogs out for a run, but then I see as it wasn't nobody I knowed.'

'Man or woman?'

'It wasn't one of the ladies, nohow. Whoever it was, they was dressed in a big coat and had a black hat well pulled down, but they was too far off, the garden, as you will know, sir, being what you might call –'

'Spacious? All right. Now what did you do next?'

'Well, I thinks to myself that, if folks was about in the garden, maybe the ladies was up, so I sneaks myself round to the back door again with me rabbits, but, blow me! – if it wasn't still locked and not a sound to be heard nowhere, without you don't count the chirping as the birds was kicking up.'

Wondering what was the best thing to do, and doubtful whether to leave the rabbits on the back doorstep, he had crept into the bushes and decided to wait until the coast – 'meaning them two as was talking' – was clear. He had needed to wait, it seemed, for some time. Apart from the fact that he was lingering

in a garden where, it would appear, he had no right to be,
another point which did not escape Burfield was that,
although the man from the loft might well have sought night
shelter during rough, wintry weather, he was not very likely to
have risked doing so on somebody else's premises on a warm
summer night and at a season when there was plenty of dry,
springy heather to furnish a bed on the moor. He said nothing
of this, but told Adams to get to the end of the story and make
it snappy.

'I can't wait to hear what happened to the rabbits,' he said
sardonically.

Because the postman, among other callers, had always
refused to walk through the grounds to the house in case the
two bitches, Isis and Nephthys, were loose, a large box had
been erected outside the main gates. It was not only roomy
enough to take the mail, including parcels, but was used by
the butcher, the baker, the milkman and so forth. It had
occurred to Adams that the rabbits could also be accommo-
dated in it.

'So that's where I left 'em,' he said, 'soon as I could see me
way clear.'

'Did the other two go off together?'

'No, they never. They seemed to be having a barney,
though they kept their voices down low, I suppose not wishing
to be 'eard from the 'ouse.'

'Did the tramp appear to be threatening the woman?'

'I never said as how the one with a hat was a woman, did
I? – though, from the way it was waving its arms about, it
could of been. Anyway, they never went off together. Him as I
thought was the tramp went first, then t'other one waited a
bit while I goes to ground deeper be'ind me bushes in case that
one had it in mind to go past me up to the house, but they
never. They undone the door of that there shed where the dog
was and took her out and down to the big gates like they was
going off for a walk. I gives 'em a few minutes, then I sneaks
down to the gates meself, parks me rabbits in the postbox and

goes off home to me bit of bread and bacon.'

'Did you see either of the others again?'

'No, I never see nobody, but one on 'em – the one in the noospaper – must have gone down the river path to Watersmeet, mustn't they? Whether t'other 'un went there, too, I couldn't say. Any road, I goed to the inquest, having a special interest, as you might say.'

'What special interest?'

'Why, sir, me recognising that there corpse as was took out of the river. I see the picture in a paper as I found in a litter bin down to Abbots Bay, so then I thinks to come to you, sir, and tell you what I seen, sir.' He looked hopefully at Burfield. The inspector said, 'But what you've told me is useless unless you can put a name to the corpse. You saw both these people –'

'And seen them chinwagging together like they was having some sort of a argyment, sir. Ain't that worth something?'

'Not to me. Did the dog go willingly with the person who took her out of her kennel?'

'Seemed to.'

'Then it must have been one of the Rant ladies or that woman who helps with the dogs.'

'I don't hardly reckon so, sir. It's true I was some way off from them while I was in the bushes, but I reckon I would have recognised one of them three.'

'They paid you for the rabbits later on, I suppose?'

'Always paid up like clockwork, sir. I haven't got nothing again' any of them ladies.'

'Exactly,' said Burfield, but the dryness of this agreement was lost upon Adams. He still looked hopeful and expectant. Burfield took out a five-pound note and handed it to him. 'Oh, well, keep your eyes and ears open, especially when you're at the Crozier Arms,' he said. 'By the way, isn't that a new shirt you're wearing? How come?'

'Give me by a charitable lady what's husband had died soon after he bought it, sir. "Do for the winter," she says, "being pure wool," she says. I put it on special to come and see *you*, sir.'

'Oh, ah? Well, I believe you, although some wouldn't. I can't see you going into a shop and buying a shirt of that quality. Just watch your step, though, that's all.'

He dismissed the poacher and then looked across at the sergeant, whom he had called in as soon as he realised that Adams had something to tell. The sergeant stood up.

'Shall I type out my shorthand, sir?'

'Oh, yes. It might come in useful later on, although I'm hanged if it tells us much at present. What did you make of his yarn?'

'I reckon it was the truth, sir, as far as it went. I don't think he's capable of making up a story like that. The only thing I'd be doubtful about –'

'Don't tell me. Give me three guesses.'

'I think you'll make do with one, sir.'

'Here goes, then. You think he *does* know who took that dog for a walk that morning.'

'Well, that's what I would bet on, sir. He came here for what he could get, but those Rant ladies are good customers of his and he wasn't going to give one of them away.'

'Right. Well, I shan't tackle him about that at present, but I wouldn't mind hearing what the ladies themselves have to say.'

'Might perhaps ask whether anything is missing from the house, sir.'

'They would have reported that.'

'Where do you think he set his snares for the rabbits, sir? There are burrows in that bank by the woods that border the river. Could he have been at Watersmeet that morning and *seen* something? I got the impression that he reckons one of the parties murdered the other. If so, he may have something to go on. He did say he thought the parties were having an argument in the garden.'

'If every argument led to murder there would be precious few of us left alive. One major point strikes me, but it is one I may be able to check with the Rant ladies.'

'Whether the morning Adams took the rabbits round to Crozier Lodge was the day the kennel-maid found the dead man in the river? Depends upon how fresh the rabbits were when one of the ladies found them in the postbox, I suppose.'

'I wonder if they'd know a fresh-killed bunny from one that had gone a bit niffy. They probably wouldn't bother much. I don't expect those hounds would object to a bit of a high flavour.'

'Anyway, in this weather, rabbit would begin to go off pretty soon, wouldn't it? Wonder whether he skinned and cleaned them before he took them round there?'

'Hardly likely, if he went to Crozier Lodge directly he'd taken them out of the snares. Ladies that breed dogs wouldn't burke at skinning and gutting a few rabbits. Very likely kept the liver and heart and kidneys to make soup for themselves.'

'I had a Boxer once and the handbook said to give the rabbit, skin and all, to him, occasional like. It made it more interesting for the dog.'

'Oh, well, it takes all sorts,' said Burfield. 'Let me have a copy of that as soon as you've typed it out. There may be something in it that, so far, we're missing.'

7

Trouble at Crozier Lodge

Laura was walking her two dogs, so Dame Beatrice herself took the call. It was Bryony Rant on the telephone.

'Sorry to bother you again,' she said, 'but we are having an awful time. At least, poor Susan is, and if it's not Susan, it could be one of us, and if it's not one of us, it must be somebody else, and that's worrying, too, because we have no idea who it could be. Of course, the man who went to the police may be lying. There are people in the village who don't like us because of father, and I daresay they don't like Susan because she works for us and tends to keep herself to herself.'

'Would you care to come over this afternoon to tell me more of the matter? In a nutshell, what is at the root of it?'

'I don't want to speak the word over the telephone. We'll be with you at half-past three.'

When Laura came in, Dame Beatrice told her about the telephone call.

'Well, there is only one word she wouldn't like to say over the telephone,' was Laura's comment, 'and that word is *murder*.'

'You jump to conclusions, do you not?'

'In this case I hardly think so. I can't wait to hear what the Rants have to say, but perhaps they panic easily.'

'Perhaps they do. We shall soon know what is troubling them and then we can make up our minds whether their panic is justified. Bryony certainly sounded agitated.'

The Rant sisters arrived to time and the story was unfolded.

Police had called at Crozier Lodge, having notified their intention of doing so and requesting that Susan be there with the
sisters and that the hounds should be under strict control
during the visit. A man in plain clothes, accompanied by
another, had identified himself as Detective-Inspector Harrow
and his companion as Detective-Sergeant Callum. They had
been polite, but their questions were penetrating and they had
been persistent in checking and re-checking the answers they
had been given.

The three women had been questioned separately and that,
said Bryony, was frightening in itself, since it was clear, in
every case, that the police did not intend to allow the other two
to hear what the third one had to say, although all had consulted together after the police had gone. They had exchanged
stories and it seemed that the questions to the Rants had
followed the same pattern.

'On the morning when your kennel-maid found that man
in the river, at what time did you first see her?'

'At about a quarter to seven,' said Bryony. Morpeth put it at
nearer half-past six, but this slight difference of opinion could
be ignored.

'Was it her usual time?'

'Yes. She came regularly at about that time.'

'How long had you been up and about?' It turned out that
Morpeth had been up first and had already begun to prepare
breakfast when Bryony came downstairs.

'Did you go into the garden before Miss Susan arrived?'

Separately, both sisters had denied having crossed the
threshold until they had heard from Susan that the Labrador
bitch was missing from her shed and did not appear to be
anywhere in the grounds.

'Were you aware that a man had spent the night in the room
above your garage?'

'Good heavens, no!' said Bryony, but when it came to
Morpeth's turn to answer the same question, she said she
wondered whether that would account for the prowler.

'Prowler? Yes, miss, we've heard mention of this prowler. Can you tell us anything about him?'

'He creeps up to the house at night just before we go to bed and taps on the window of the room where we are and runs away when we look out to see who it is.'

'How do you know it's a man? You have a doctor's brass plate on your front gates, we noticed. Could it not have been a woman seeking medical advice – a summer holiday visitor who did not know that a doctor no longer lives at Crozier Lodge? – your late father, wasn't it?'

Morpeth admitted that this was so, but she doubted whether the window-tapper was a would-be patient because, in that case, surely the caller would have knocked on the door or returned in the morning to ask for help, whereas nothing of the kind had happened and they had had to put up with the nuisance for several nights in succession. Bryony had also rejected the suggestion that the unwanted visitor was a woman.

'It never gets really dark when the skies are clear at this time of year,' she said. 'We saw him run off and he ran like a man. Besides, I don't believe a woman would come prowling round the house and tapping on windows. It isn't the kind of thing women do unless you know them very well and are prepared to let them use such informality. We are on no such terms with anybody, not even Susan.'

Harrow had remarked, at this point, that it was not possible to estimate, particularly in these days, what women would or would not do, or to state categorically whether a woman running away with her back to the watchers could be distinguished from a man, particularly if the fugitive was wearing trousers and disappearing into the darkness of the garden bushes.

'Well, none of the village women would venture to enter the grounds, even by daylight,' said Bryony. 'As for Susan, why should she come and haunt us at bedtime?'

'She is in your mind, though, miss, or you wouldn't have mentioned her. As for anybody else, man or woman, I suppose they would take it for granted that your dogs would be shut away by night.'

'Why should they? Lots of people have guard dogs which are let loose to roam the garden at night. We don't, because our hounds are too valuable for us to risk having them stolen. There's only Sekhmet left loose and she is hardly worth stealing and certainly would be no use as a guard dog. She's a fool and trusts everybody.'

'Yet, according to the story we heard before the inquest and, again, at it, somebody may have made an attempt to steal her, miss, and that brings me to my next point. Our information is that somebody took the Labrador out very much earlier than usual on the day in question and the inference is that, when your kennel-maid reported the dog was missing, it had been gone for only about an hour or less, and had been taken out for a run, it seemed, by a so-far unidentified person.'

'Well, I can assure you none of us took her out that morning.'

'Are you sure you did not take her out yourself that morning, miss, and leave her at Watersmeet and get yourself back to the house before the kennel-maid showed up?'

Both sisters had been firm in denying that they had left the house before breakfast that morning. Bryony dismissed the suggestion as ludicrous; Morpeth had asked plaintively why anybody should think either of them would depart so far from custom as to take that particular dog out at all.

'Poor old Sekhmet hardly ever gets a run like the hounds,' she said. 'She has all the grounds to roam and we take it in turns to play with her, throwing sticks or a ball. She never lacks exercise and we all go miles with the hounds each day and really couldn't do with any more walking.'

When the police had done with the Rant sisters it had been Susan's turn. Bryony reported to Dame Beatrice what Susan had told them of the interview.

'They asked Morpeth and me in turn to show them our hats,' said Bryony, 'but, of course, neither of us ever wears a hat. A headscarf is the most we ever aspire to. Perhaps we would have hats if we ever went to church, but we never do go to church. I daresay Susan goes to early service on Sundays because she was brought up in Axehead vicarage and she is never here before about half-past nine every Sunday. We, Morpeth and I, have a long lie-in on that day of the week, but Susan's adoptive father was the vicar of Axehead, Abbots Bay and Abbots Crozier, so she may have formed a childhood habit of Sunday churchgoing that she can't break. On the other hand, she also may think a long lie-in is her due on Sundays, as she is up so early during the rest of the week. We have never asked any questions. We give her breakfast when she turns up, having had ours a little earlier. As a matter of fact, Morpeth is usually out with a couple of the hounds when Susan gets here on Sundays, so I sit in the kitchen and chat with Susan while she has her bacon and egg.'

'And you do not possess a hat of any kind?' asked Dame Beatrice.

'Neither of us does, and I can't imagine Susan ever wears one, even for church. Customs have changed over that sort of conventional thing. I am told that some of the holidaymakers turn up in trousers, although the present incumbent has had a strong word to say in the parish magazine about shorts and bras.'

'Do the summer visitors read the parish magazine?' asked Laura, who was also present at the conference.

'I shouldn't think so,' Bryony admitted, 'but perhaps they get the message in other ways. Anyway, the vicar can hardly preach a sermon about such women's matters, although he did nip a nudist colony in the bud down at Abbots Bay last summer.'

'The vicar couldn't preach a sermon about women in bras and shorts?' said Laura. 'I bet he would if he dared. I could give him his text, too. How about the seventh chapter of Proverbs, verse ten?'

'We don't know much about the Old Testament,' said Bryony.

'You've missed a treat. Great stuff. I was brought up on it.

May I quote?' Without waiting for the consent or otherwise of
her hearers, Laura continued, 'Authorised Version, of course.
To my mind, there is no other worth reading. ''Behold, there
met him a woman with the attire of an harlot.'' My word!
What wouldn't I give to be in the pulpit with a text like that
under my belt with which to wallop the ungodly! But perhaps,
if the vicar used a text like that to rebuke the female holidaymakers, he might stir up the disapproval of another Jeanie
Deans.'

'People don't bring their own stools to church nowadays,'
said Morpeth.

'There are always hassocks,' returned Laura.

'We began by mentioning hats,' said Dame Beatrice.
'What had hats to do with the visit from the police?'

'I don't know. They didn't say. They didn't really tell us
anything. They asked very politely whether we would allow the
sergeant to inspect the whole of the house. They admitted they
hadn't got a search warrant. I don't know what Morpeth
thought –'

'It scared me,' said Morpeth. 'It looked as though they
though I was telling a lie when I said I didn't possess a hat.
Anyway, it was better not to put obstacles in their way, so I said
that, if Bryony agreed to it, I had no objection whatever to
letting them search the house.'

'I said the same,' said Bryony. 'I wasn't exactly scared, but I
was a bit worried. Surely they couldn't really have been looking for hats? I thought they were after something else,
although I had no idea what it could be. However, the sergeant came back after what seemed a long time and spoke to
the other officer, so the police must doubt the verdict given at
the inquest and are following up a clue of some sort, I suppose.'

'Did you hear what was said after the sergeant had searched
the house?'

'No. They moved apart from me and spoke in undertones,
but I think it was to the effect that the sergeant had not found

hats or anything else he had been looking for. They went away after they had seen Susan, but I don't believe they were satisfied. I watched them out of the window and they went in the direction of the garage. It wasn't on their way to the gate, so I don't know what they wanted with it. We keep it locked, but they didn't ask for the key.'

'Do you think they had come upon some information which had caused them to visit you?'

'Well, of course, it was not our first visit from the police. We had an inspector called Burfield after Susan found the body. He was in uniform, but these two plain-clothes men were detectives and we didn't like that at all. As for the information, so-called, we realised where that must have come from when we remembered the five rabbits in the postbox.'

'Rabbits in the postbox?' exclaimed Laura.

'Oh, dead ones, of course,' said Morpeth. 'Adams, the village poacher, had put them there, the day Sekhmet disappeared. We told Susan to give him his money if he called while we were out. He must have come up to the house with them early in the morning, I suppose, and thought it was too early to knock us up.'

'Other times he left some rabbits in the kitchen,' said Morpeth, 'but he couldn't do that this time because we lock the back door every night since we had the prowler.'

'So this poacher saw something he thought suspicious and went to the police,' said Dame Beatrice. 'If the man is a hunter of illicit fish or game, it seems a strange thing for him to have done.'

'Oh, Adams would do anything for the sake of a ten-pence piece,' said Bryony. 'Besides, although he has been up before the magistrates in Axehead a couple of times, he has never been convicted of anything.'

'Is there any reason why he should want to make trouble?'

'I'm sure there isn't. His rabbits are useful because they make a change of diet for the hounds and we always pay him promptly.'

'So you think that he really did see whatever he seems to have mentioned to the police?'

'Well, you know, Susan was very doubtful about that inquest. She said the man would have kicked Sekhmet, not given the dog his trousers. But I do think Adams could have come and told us that he was going to the police with information and then left us to deal with the matter. Is there anything you can do to get the police off our backs? I'm sure they suspect murder, as Susan does.'

'Has this poacher a home?'

'Yes. He lives in a bivouac sort of shelter on the moor about three miles from our house.'

Between them, the sisters described the location of Adams' shack.

'Am I likely to find him at home at about midday tomorrow?' asked Dame Beatrice. 'I should like to hear what he has to say. Of course, he may not have been the cause of the visit from the police.'

'He will be in the Crozier Arms at midday tomorrow,' said Bryony. 'He goes there most days when he has any money.'

'Excellent. My chauffeur shall waylay him there. Meanwhile, I think I ought to talk with your kennel-maid. I heard what she had to say at the inquest, but I may gain a pointer or two in private conversation. Will she still be at Crozier Lodge if we set off immediately?'

'I doubt it. If we are not there, she won't stay once she has shut the hounds in the stable yard.'

'Then we will have tea and I will visit her tomorrow after I have heard from George whether the poacher has anything to say. How is George to identify him at the Crozier Arms?'

'He is always accompanied by a lurcher bitch when he goes to the pub. If he gets into an argument it is handy to have her with him, I suppose. She bit my father once, when father lanced a boil on Adams' neck,' said Morpeth.

'Will you lunch with us tomorrow?' asked Bryony, after a pause during which she had caught her sister's eye and telegraphed a message.

'Thank you, no. While George is talking to Adams, we shall

pay a visit to the Headlands hotel and lunch there, while we make some enquiries about Mr Goodfellow. You have heard no more of him, I suppose?'

'Not a thing,' replied Bryony.

'Unless he was our prowler,' said Morpeth. Her sister glanced at her. 'Well, he was dotty enough to come tapping on windows when it was nearly bedtime,' Morpeth went on, looking at Dame Beatrice for support.

'If you ask me, he wasn't dotty at all,' said Laura. 'I put him down as a right villain. All those quotations and the king of kings stuff!'

'When he asked for a doctor and you brought him to me,' said Dame Beatrice, 'did he give any indication that he was surprised at the length of the journey? I agree with Laura that he was not mentally deranged as the layman understands the term, so he must have realised that there were doctors much nearer to Abbots Crozier than the Stone House.'

'First, I suggested Dr Mortlake, but he said he had been treated by him some time before and did not care for it to happen again. Then, I'm afraid I lied and mentioned Lambridge.'

'So, if he knew Dr Mortlake, he had been in the neighbourhood before.'

'Well, he certainly knew Dr Mortlake's name. After that, I just drove on, intending, as I had done from the first, to land him on to you. I think he knew what I was doing because he pointed out the road sign to Brockenhurst and asked me if that wasn't the way.'

'Interesting. Do go on.'

'When I told him at Crozier Lodge that I would take him to a doctor, his behaviour became even more extravagant and extraordinary than it had been at first. Morpeth asked whether she should come with me. I told her to put one of the Nile gods in the back of the car. She knew what I meant, of course. Osiris, Anubis, Horus and Amon are like lambs in the ordinary course of events, but I should be very sorry if anybody turned awkward towards one of us when they were about.

'Ozymandias asked whether it was necessary to take Osiris with us. He said he was allergic to dogs. I said that they enjoyed a ride in a car, but liked people to be nice and quiet when they were about. Well, that calmed him down and, most of the journey he seemed to be asleep.'

'But he didn't miss the road signs to Brockenhurst,' said Laura. 'Well, Wandles Parva isn't far off from there.'

'No. Well, he didn't begin acting up again until we were in sight of your windows. I had to reassure Osiris and tell him it was all right.'

'I wouldn't touch her, mate,' said Adams to George when they had met and were fraternising in the Crozier Arms next day. George had paid for the beer and was making overtures towards the lurcher. 'She's obliged for the sausage you give her, but she's kind of awkward in her manners with strangers.' He stirred the crossbred affectionately with his foot and applied himself to the pint for which George had paid. 'Don't do for me to keep the dog too friendly with folks, living alone as I do and every man's hand agin me, as you might say.'

'But not the hand of the ladies at Crozier Lodge,' said George, 'or so you were telling me.'

'Oh, them! Born innocent and never got over it.'

'I heard the police had been there. That doesn't sound much like innocence. What have they been up to?'

'Well, that's a funny kind of a tale, that is.'

'Let's have a snack and another drink. I'm on a newspaper, so I can do with a funny kind of tale.'

'A noospaper? Any dough attached?'

'Depends on the story. If the story is worth anything to me, the paper might go as far as a tenner.'

'I thought noospapers paid thousands.'

'Only for a real scoop, and then it's got to be in one of the big dailies. Anyway, please yourself.' He ordered pasties and another couple of pints and led the way to a small table.

Adams picked up a clean beer-mat and put it in his pocket.

'Different to last week,' he said. 'I got quite a collection. Shall flog it when I gets the right bid for it. Bound to be somebody interested, with all this holiday lot about.'

'I used to collect paper hats when I was a kid and got invited to parties,' said George, who had been well briefed by Dame Beatrice. 'Paper hats and mottoes out of Christmas crackers. I reckon I finished up with enough funny jokes to keep a low comedian going for life. As for hats –'

'Funny you should mention hats.' Adams, between mouthfuls of pasty and great slurps of beer, told the story of his experiences in the grounds of Crozier Lodge. 'So I ain't surprised as the fuzz been nosing around there,' he concluded.

'I thought he well deserved a reward, madam,' said George to Dame Beatrice later, 'so I made it a few pounds and, of course, his refreshments. I hope that's all right, madam.'

'Good old George!' said Laura, when the chauffeur, in civvies for the occasion, had left them in the lounge of the Headlands hotel. 'At least we know now why the police went hat-hunting at Crozier Lodge. I suppose by this time they've been to the kennel-maid's cottage and had a look-round there.'

'I imagine so. If the story this man Adams told to George is true, it seems to have been a strange time of day and, apparently, an unprecedented circumstance, for anybody to have taken Sekhmet out for exercise.'

'Yes, it certainly wasn't one of the Rants because it was at Watersmeet that Susan found the dog. It must have gone off with a stranger. They have always said that Sekhmet will trust anybody and is amiable to the point of idiocy.'

'It was not one of the Rant sisters, perhaps,' said Dame Beatrice, 'but what interests me is whether Susan left her cottage at the usual time that morning or much earlier.'

'And took Sekhmet out and left her at Watersmeet with the stinking aniseed on some trousers to keep her happy, so that she knew perfectly well the dog wouldn't be in that garden shed when she visited it later? Sounds far-fetched to me. Why should she do such a thing?'

'Time will tell whether she did do such a thing. Let us go to Crozier Lodge and talk to Susan. They will have finished lunch by now.'

'I thought you wanted to talk to the hotel people here at the Headlands about Mr Ozymandias.'

'Useless, and only an excuse to get out of having lunch with the Rant sisters. Bryony invited us, but I noted the consternation on Morpeth's face and then her expression of relief when the invitation was refused. Incidentally, it seemed to me that Bryony's story yesterday confirmed my suspicion that Goodfellow knew perfectly well that she was taking him to see me and that his disorientated performance at Crozier Lodge was directed towards that end and is now explained.'

Susan was out with two of the hounds when Laura and Dame Beatrice called at Crozier Lodge. The sisters said that she hated meeting strangers and would probably put Osiris and Horus back into the stable yard and go straight home rather than stay and talk with the visitors.

'She even went to the length of making us promise not to tell you where she lived,' said Bryony.

'So we promised, of course, and shall have to keep to it,' said Morpeth. 'Anyway, although we know more or less where the cottage is, we have never been to it, so we couldn't give you an address, even if we wanted to.'

Susan returned to the house after Dame Beatrice and Laura had gone to their own home, but Dame Beatrice had left an urgent message and was not surprised when Bryony arrived at the Stone House with Susan late that same evening.

'We didn't want to leave our place empty,' said Bryony, 'because of the hounds, so Morpeth is staying, but Susan wants to see you because of the message you left with me. I hope this won't take too long. Morpeth is very nervous about being left alone so late in the evening.'

'Then I suggest that you return at once and when Susan has

consulted us we will give her a bed for the night. George will take Susan straight back after an early breakfast.'

'Decent of you,' said Susan, in the gruff, unfriendly tone to which the sisters were accustomed, but which new acquaintances found singularly unattractive and boorish, although Dame Beatrice knew that it was an indication of almost unconquerable shyness and a lack of self-confidence. 'In a spot of bother. Glad of some advice.'

Laura looked at the square, strongly built figure, the athletic balance on the balls of the large feet, the weather-beaten face with its powerful jaw and the bare forearms muscled like those of a coal-heaver, and summed Susan up as not a person she would want to meet in a dark alley if Susan had any reason to dislike her.

Dame Beatrice saw an obstinate, rather stupid woman, but one who, underneath a belligerent exterior, was as frightened as a bewildered child. She said briskly, 'That's settled, then. A cup of coffee, since Bryony will not wish to drink and drive, and you should have Susan back, my dear Bryony, in good time in the morning, although later than usual because of the length of the journey and, of course, my chauffeur's beauty sleep.'

8

Kennel-Maid

'The police have an awful way of making you feel you've got a guilty conscience,' said Susan, when Bryony had gone.

'It's the basis of all the brainwashing techniques,' said Laura. 'Once an interrogator can get the guilt complex going, the rest is easy.'

'Everybody has a guilty conscience, if they have a conscience at all,' said Dame Beatrice. 'I am inclined to think that consciences of the kind we mean do not exist in some of the present generation. To what aspect of your own conscience did the police appeal?'

It appeared that the cat and mouse dialogue which had taken place between Susan and Detective-Inspector Harrow with Detective-Sergeant Callum taking notes had hinged first of all on the time factor.

'What time did you get up here to Crozier Lodge that particular morning, miss, when you saw the body in the river?'

'The usual time, somewhere between six and half-past. I don't know exactly, but, yes, much as usual. The others will tell you if you ask them.'

'You were seen to leave your cottage at just before five, miss. Does it really take you more than an hour to get from there to Abbots Crozier?'

'Of course not. I did leave the cottage just about five. I went for a bathe in the pool. I often do at this time of year. I came up to Crozier Lodge after I was dried and dressed.'

'Would you mind telling us what you were wearing when you went for your swim, miss?'

'My cottage is quite near the pool, so I had a rainproof over my bikini and rope-soled shoes on my feet.'

'No hat, miss?'

'Why on earth should I need a hat? My hair is short, so I don't even wear a swimming cap. I just wash the salt water out when I get home. Anyway, I don't possess a hat.'

'You were seen to leave your cottage, but you did not return to it until the evening after you had spent the usual day here at Crozier Lodge.'

'Because I wasn't *seen* to go back after my swim does not mean that I *didn't* go back, does it?'

'There was a man fishing off the jetty early in the morning, miss. He swears there was nobody in the pool before seven.'

'He wouldn't be looking towards the pool if he was on the end of the jetty.'

'There was another chap, a holidaymaker, out with a local boatman. They didn't see anybody in the pool, either.'

'Why should they? The sea wall round the pool is quite high and their boat would have been a long way offshore.'

'When you got to Crozier Lodge, miss, did you meet a man in the garden before you went up to the house?'

'Certainly not. I should soon have asked him his business if I had. Nobody ever comes up to the house. Isis and Nephthys are often loose in the garden and people round here are afraid of the hounds.'

'Would you have any objection to accompanying us to your cottage, miss, and letting us have a look round?'

'Oh, Lord! It's in a bit of a mess. I'm not a very tidy person and I hate housework.'

'We're not critics of housekeeping, miss. We have no authority to search your premises, but it might look a bit like obstruction if you refuse to give us the facilities we ask for.'

'Is that a threat?'

'No, miss. I'll come clean with you. We are by no means satisfied with the verdict which was given at the inquest and nor are a lot of people. Matters have been brought to our notice which need some explaining. We shall get at the truth in the end, but meanwhile a bit of co-operation from anybody who is in a position to help us will be welcome.'

'But I'm not in a position to help you. I don't know a thing except that I was unlucky enough to be the person who found that man's body in the river and, because of that, I've been hounded and harassed ever since. It's most unfair.'

'From what we have been told, you did alter one of your usual habits, miss. Instead of going straight up to this house, you went to a shed in the garden to look at one of the dogs. Why did you do that?'

'I thought I heard Sekhmet whining. I thought there might be something wrong with her.'

'And you found she wasn't there at all, so you could hardly have heard her whining.'

'When I found she wasn't there I went up to the house to tell Bryony and Morpeth – to tell the two Miss Rants – and then I went straight off to search for the dog. That's when I found that drowned man. And I *did* go swimming earlier, whether anybody saw me or not.'

'So, of course, we went to my cottage,' said Susan to Dame Beatrice. 'There was no reason for me to refuse. When we got there, the first thing the detective said was that he had noticed I didn't keep my back door locked when I was out. I had taken them in by the back way because I always go in and out by the back door. My front door faces the sea, so the back door's that much nearer the cliff path. Nobody locks up in Abbots Bay until bedtime. There is nothing in my cottage worth stealing, anyway.'

'Did they find any hats?' asked Laura.

'As a matter of fact, they did. The detective-inspector stayed with me downstairs while his sergeant did the searching. There was a hat on the shelf in my wardrobe and, what I suppose they thought was worse, a piece of cloth which could be part of the waistband of a pair of trousers, although it could have been from a skirt. I insisted that the hat was not mine and I put it on to prove my point. Talk about a pimple on a doughnut! It could have been a doll's hat when I perched it on my head. You will notice that I have a big, wide cranium. Well, the hat just perched on top of it, as I said. There is a mirror in my sitting-room, so, when I had put it on at their request, I took a peep. Honestly, you never saw anything so ridiculous.'

The police, Susan went on to say, were forced to believe that the hat need not be her property. She suggested that it had been planted on her and pointed out that they had seen for themselves that anybody could enter the cottage while she was out of it during the daylight hours and she added that, if the hat had been left in the cottage, the piece of trousering could have been left at the same time.

'They had to admit that this could be true,' she said, 'but they stuck to their point that, although I had been seen to leave the cottage earlier than I had admitted when they talked to me on the day I found the body, I could give them no proof that I had gone for a swim and then had tramped up to Crozier Lodge at my usual time.'

'And did the piece of cloth provide any evidence?' asked Dame Beatrice.

'No. It was the same colour and, from what I could remember, the same material as the trousers Sekhmet was guarding when I found her and the dead man, but there was no maker's mark or anything else on it. There seemed no reason why anybody should have chopped it out of the waistband, still less why I should have pushed it into a drawer where the sergeant said he found it.'

'I believe you know a man by the name of Adams who lives on the moor. Has this Adams any reason to wish harm to you?'

'Not so far as I know. I don't personally pay him for the rabbits he gives the Rants or provide him with any food, but I have always called Bryony or Morpeth when he comes to Crozier Lodge, so he never goes away with empty pockets or an empty belly. I can't do more than that. It isn't my business to pay him or feed him.'

There was a long pause before Dame Beatrice said very gently, 'You did not really go for a swim that morning.'

Susan looked at her sharply and then at Laura. An expression of mulish obstinacy came over her large, unattractive countenance. Her small, green eyes became wary and her heavy jaw was firmly set. When she spoke, she said sullenly, 'If you're not going to believe me, we may as well leave it at that.'

'I am always prepared to listen to the truth,' said Dame Beatrice. 'It is clear that you were seen to leave the cottage at a very early hour that morning. It is equally clear that unbiased persons, who had every opportunity to do so, did not see you in the pool, and nobody saw you return to the cottage until the evening.'

'How do you know the fisherman and the man in the boat were unbiased? Everybody makes enemies. There are people around who don't like me much.'

'Why don't you come clean with us?' demanded Laura. 'Seems to me you're in a bit of a spot. *We* don't dislike you. Open up and stop gumming the works.'

'That's what that damned policeman said. Well, it amounted to that. He said he would tell me something they had found out from Adams. He said Adams had told them he had gone early to Crozier Lodge with some rabbits for the hounds, but, as nobody was up and about, he had left them in the postbox because the back door was locked, so he couldn't get into the kitchen. Well, that was true enough. Bryony found the rabbits when she went down to take in the milk. What may or may not be true is the rest of Adams' story.'

'You mean that Adams told the police that he had seen two people talking together in the grounds of Crozier Lodge that morning? We had that story from my chauffeur, who met Adams in the Crozier Arms,' said Dame Beatrice. 'I sent him to make an enquiry about hats, but he came back with a tale of five rabbits. Oh, well, there is an established connection between hats and rabbits, as every amateur conjurer knows.'

'A rabbit might eat the hat the detective-sergeant found in

my cottage,' said Susan, perking up as though she felt an easing of the tension. 'It was made of straw.'

'Whereas, according to the description of it which Adams gave to George, the hat worn in the garden of Crozier Lodge was likely to have been of felt or tweed. Can you think of anybody who might have been calling so early in the morning?'

'No, I can't. Nobody ever calls. They're afraid of the Pharaohs.'

'A strange man who gave me his name as Robin Goodfellow also claims to be a Pharaoh. He introduced himself at first as Ozymandias, king of kings, as in Shelley's poem.'

'Oh, yes, the Rants have mentioned him once or twice. They thought he was a nutcase. Whether he was or not, he was a stranger in the place or he would never have dared to walk up to the door. As for Adams, well, so far as his story goes, I think he could have made the whole thing up. He's quite capable of inventing a tissue of lies. He's lied himself out of trouble often enough when he's been charged with poaching.'

'I see no reason, though, why he should lie in the circumstances we are discussing. He saw what may have been two strangers in the Rants' grounds and he had a legitimate reason for being in the grounds himself that morning. The rabbits the Rant sisters found in their postbox are proof of it.'

'Oh, as to rabbits, if he can't supply them – and we don't always get them, even when he's got any, because he can get a better price for prime young plump ones from the butcher in Axehead – we can always purchase them elsewhere.'

'Elsewhere?'

'Yes, elsewhere. The hounds are partial to rabbit.'

'Will you tell me how you came to team up with the Rant sisters?'

'By accident, in a way.'

'We also came to know them by accident, or, rather, because of an accident in which their car was involved.'

'Mine wasn't that kind of accident; it was because of a row in a shop between the shopkeeper and Morpeth. Had Bryony been there, I would not have been needed, but Morpeth is not very tough and the shopkeeper turned bad-tempered with her. Can't remember what it was all about, but I think she had brought back a chicken which was getting a bit too ripe. The tradesmen won't go to Crozier Lodge, otherwise Bryony would soon send the goods to the rightabout if they weren't up to sample; so poor old Morpeth gets the job of taking anything back to the shop if it isn't what's wanted because mostly she is the one who has been fobbed off with it in the first place.'

'So you came to her rescue in this instance?'

'Yes. Then we got into conversation and the upshot was that I went back with her to Crozier Lodge and offered to help with the hounds and they accepted.'

'Up to that time, your time was your own, I take it. I wonder how you occupied yourself before you joined forces with the two sisters? Were you alone in the world?'

Susan told her story. She and her elder brother had been orphaned at a very early age – or else they had been born on the wrong side of the blanket. Whichever it was, they had been taken into care by the county authority and, later, Susan had been separated from her brother, fostered and then adopted by the late vicar of Axehead Abbots Bay and Abbots Crozier. When his wife died she had looked after the ageing man, and on his retirement in favour of a younger incumbent had moved with him into a local cottage, which he had since left to her by will. She had continued to live in the cottage after his death.

What money he left also came to her and, although it was not much, it brought her a tiny income which she had eked out by doing casual work, sometimes fruit picking or other harvesting jobs, sometimes as a domestic help, sometimes working in the hotels in Abbots Bay and Abbots Crozier.

'So you knew all about the Rant sisters before you joined them,' said Dame Beatrice.

'I knew their father got himself a bad name because a couple of his patients died. There was a lot of trouble about one of them in particular. You hear so much gossip when you go from one job to another, as I was doing. There were rumours that Dr Rant had had to leave his practice in the Midlands for much the same kind of reason and, of course, that story blossomed and it was suspected that the Midlands patient had been conned into leaving him her money. You never know where scandalmongering will stop·when once tongues start wagging.'

It was clear that the conversation had come to an end so far as Susan was concerned. Dinner was served and Susan, who had eaten her meal almost in silence, retired early to bed. On the following morning, she was sent off in the car, driven by George.

'Well,' said Laura, when she had waved Susan goodbye from the front steps of the Stone House, 'where do we go from here? If she didn't go swimming that morning, where *did* she go?'

'I think we had better take it as a working hypothesis that she may have gone to Crozier Lodge, that there she may have met this man who had spent the night in the room above the garage, and that then she may have taken Sekhmet to Watersmeet and left her there –'

'And on the excuse of going to look for the dog, she could have met the man again and killed him?'

'I do not know. If she did, it will be necessary for the police to find out what previous connection they had had with one another. Until the man is identified, that will be impossible, I think.'

'The non-fit hat and the useless piece of trouser-band could have been planted by Susan herself for the police to find, I suppose,' said Laura. 'She could prove the hat was quite the wrong size and the bit of material gave nothing away. If it was proved that she *did* plant them with intention to deceive, that would about cook her goose.'

'I think I would like a word with the poacher myself. Now that George has paved the way with largesse, the man should not be unwilling to talk to me.'

Dame Beatrice refused to have Laura accompany her to the shack and timed her arrival for four in the afternoon – an hour, she decided, when all sensible poachers and other night-birds would be at home catching up on their sleep.

Adams came to the door with the lurcher at his heels and no very friendly expression on his face. He said in surly tones that he did not want any magazines or tracts and was C. of E. Dame Beatrice cackled and said that her own prejudice concerning religious literature coincided with his and, indicating the briefcase she was carrying, added that all she had come for was an exchange of opinions concerning the Rant sisters and any information about them which he was willing to supply.

'For a consideration, of course,' she added. 'I hope that you possess two chairs which you are prepared to place out here on the moor. One likes to be outdoors in this extremely pleasant weather.'

'Ah, the shack do stink,' he agreed. ''Tis the bitch and the rabbits, and I've had a hare hanging up. What sort of consideration would you have in mind, mum?'

'I would prefer to do that kind of thinking when I have put my questions to you. I ought to warn you that I have made contact with a journalist who interviewed you at the Crozier Arms recently, so I shall be able to check your statements to some extent. I want facts, not fairytales.'

'Not over-civil, be you?'

'Bring out the chairs and let us get down to business. Neither of us, I imagine, has time to waste.'

'I wonder a little old lady like you has the nerve to come out to a place like this on your own and tell a man you reckons he's a liar, given half the chance, specially when you got money on you.'

'Oh, as to that,' said Dame Beatrice, slipping a hand into a pocket and producing a small revolver, 'I usually travel with what the American gangsters used to refer to as the old equaliser. An apt name for a gun, don't you think?'

At this he grinned, saluted with mock ceremonial, went

indoors and a few moments later they were seated out on the moors with bees busy in the early heather of the south-west and the flies rising in the bracken. The lurcher remained indoors, shut away from the conference.

Whether it was because she had already heard the story from George or for some other reason, Adams repeated to Dame Beatrice what he had told the so-called reporter and, incidentally, what he had told the police, although he did not mention this. When she had heard the account, she began to question him. The poacher answered readily enough, although he told her that most of his knowledge had been gained by hearsay and not by personal experience. 'Me not having no sort of use for a doctor,' he explained. 'When I got anything wrong I cures it meself, same like me father before me. Never knoo me mother. I don't reckon her and me dad was ever married –'

'Yes, now to get back to the matter in hand. It could have been a woman you saw with the man who had slept in the loft above the Rants' garage –'

'Wot of it? I can only tell you what I told the police. I don't know who it was.'

'To have been up and about so early, the person must have lived locally, and a villager, from what I have been told, would not have ventured into the garden of Crozier Lodge.'

'I ent saying nothing about that. I was too far away to spot who it was. That's to say, if I had knowed 'em anyway. I didn't call nobody to mind as they reminded me of, though.'

'This other person, the one you found in the loft, did he remind you of anybody you knew?'

'Not as I recollects.'

'It seems to me that he must have known the house. He would not otherwise have realised that the loft was available for occupation. Was Dr Rant the village physician when you were younger?'

'Him? Cor! Even if I was a-dying, I wouldn't never have gone to that murdering sod.'

9

Poacher and Doctor

'The noun,' said Dame Beatrice, 'I will ignore. The adjective I find intriguing. Whom did Dr Rant murder? – and under what circumstances?'

'Is it worth a fiver to you?'

'We shall both know that when I have heard the story.'

'What do you want to know for?'

'Because this death at Watersmeet may well lead to a charge of murder against person or persons so far unknown.'

'Dr Rant couldn't a-done it. He'm dead.'

'I believe, though, that certain people still harbour such a grudge against him that they have extended it towards his daughters and even to their kennel-maid. What can he have done to arouse and sustain such rancour? All doctors make mistakes at times.'

'Ah, well, one or two of *his* mistakes, folks reckons, was made a-purpose.'

'The story, if credible and well substantiated, is worth the five pounds you postulated. Fire away and do not spare the details. We have plenty of time before the Crozier Arms opens its hospitable doors to you.'

Beyond emphasising that he had obtained his information by what he referred to as 'pub talk', Adams told his story as though he had personal knowledge of its details.

After the death of his wife, Dr Rant had taken to the bottle, but this, it was surmised, was not so much because of his loss – there might have been sympathetic understanding for that – but because two of his patients had died when, in the opinion of the 'old wives' of the village, who included in their number the village midwife, the first of the patients should have recovered.

The inquest that followed the death of Dr Rant himself found that, fuddled by drink, he had taken an overdose of the drug he had prescribed for himself and died from the combined effects of the drug and the alcohol. It was pointed out by the medical witnesses that a doctor, of all people, should have known the danger of combining the two, and there was some talk that the truer verdict would have been one of suicide.

When the doctor's will was proved, the bulk of the money and the house itself had been left to Bryony and Morpeth. However, Dr Rant's younger partner, who had 'lived in' at Crozier Lodge for several years, received a sufficiently handsome sum to buy his own practice in Abbots Bay. This again displeased the villagers, since they then had no doctor at all in Abbots Crozier and were obliged to go down to the other village if they needed to attend surgery.

'So what had caused the deaths of the two patients?' Dame Beatrice enquired. Adams could answer this question. One of the doctor's victims had been apprenticed to the village carpenter. While at work, the youth had dropped a chisel and made a nasty gash in his thigh. The doctor, as usual, had referred him to the hospital, but the boy demurred, so Dr Rant had stopped the bleeding and put on a dressing. Local opinion was that the dressing was unsterilised and possibly even soiled. At any rate, the wound became infected and the lad died of septicaemia.

The other case was markedly different, although it was the immediate result of the first one. The aunt of the dead apprentice went to Crozier Lodge to take Dr Rant to task because of the young man's untimely end. A bitter altercation ensued and the doctor turned the woman forcibly out of the house. She was alleged to have missed her footing on the front steps because she turned her head to shout abuse at Rant. That was the version he gave at the inquest and there was no one to dispute it, since the only other person present was a jobbing gardener who was too far away to be able to give an acceptable account of what had happened and who claimed that, until he had heard the woman scream as she fell, he had been unaware that anybody was leaving the house. The woman was concussed by the fall and died by the time the ambulance reached the Axehead hospital.

Her husband claimed that Dr Rant must have pushed her down the steps and, in his cups, although not in court, the jobbing gardener had admitted that the sounds of vituperation proceeding from the top of the front steps had been audible to him, that he had stopped work to listen and look, and that he had seen the woman come hurtling down the steps on to the concrete path below 'like she had been given a good sharp shove'.

He had dropped the garden fork he was holding and had run to where the woman lay. There was no sign of Dr Rant, although the gardener had seen him standing at the open front door only a few moments earlier. In that case, even if he had stepped inside and closed the door, he must have heard the woman scream as she fell. Finding her unconscious, the gardener had hammered on the door. This produced the elder daughter, Bryony, who looked down and saw the woman lying on the path. Bryony, according to the story, had gone indoors to find her father.

'It seems a pity,' said Dame Beatrice, 'that village animosity against their father should have spilled over on to his daughters. It savours of witch-hunting and is equally unjust.'

Adams agreed.

'Nice ladies,' he said, 'but the village has their reasons. They don't like all them dogs, for one thing, but, more than that, there's them as reckons one or other of the ladies could have testified at the inquest of Mrs Subbock, her what was killed falling down them steps. Stands to reason, says some, as the row outside the front door must have been heard by them inside the house and somebody would have looked out the window, even if they done nothing else, to see what all the palaver were about.'

'And so witnessed the accident? I take your point and I think it more than likely that you are right and that there would have been a witness to the accident – more than one witness, perhaps. However, witnesses are not always prepared to come forward, especially when their evidence may bring trouble to a member of their own family. Do you know anything about relations between the doctor and his wife?'

'Used to bash her about – the girls, too, so I heared,' said Adams, 'but it don't do to believe everything you hears. As for Dr Mortlake, now, down in Abbots Bay, as used to be Dr Rant's assistant, well, they all testified as he were out on his afternoon rounds when Mrs Subbock cracked her nut falling down them steps.'

It was Laura who telephoned Dr Mortlake.

'Dame Beatrice Lestrange Bradley's secretary here,' she said. 'Dr Mortlake?'

'Speaking. What can I do for Dame Beatrice?'

'Will you suggest a time convenient to you when you could meet? As soon as possible, please.'

'I shall be honoured to meet her, of course. Where?'

'Preferably here at the Stone House, Wandles Parva. Will you dine with us? We can put you up for the night.'

'Thanks very much. Will Wednesday suit Dame Beatrice?'

'I'm sure it will.'

'My colleague in Axehead can get a locum to take my evening surgery.'

'Right. We'll expect you at half-past seven. We dine at eight in the summer.'

'May I ask what it's all about?'

'It's Home Office business, I think.'

'Oh, really? What is that to do with me?'

'I can't tell you any more. Wednesday at half-past seven, then.'

Dr Mortlake was a clean-shaven, personable man of between thirty-five and forty, or so Dame Beatrice guessed. No mention was made of the reason for the invitation until dinner was over and the three were in the drawing-room having coffee. Dame Beatrice opened what Laura described as the business meeting by remarking that she had made the acquaintance of the Rant sisters. She then looked at Laura, who explained how this had come about. She went on to say that she believed Dr Mortlake knew them well.

'I did, at one time,' he said, 'but that was several years ago. As you probably know, I was their father's assistant for a time and I lived with the family at Crozier Lodge.'

'Mrs Rant was alive at the time, I suppose?'

'Oh, yes. She lived for a year or two years after I joined them. Rant and I each had a surgery on the ground floor – but, after he died – it must be three years ago now – I left. For one thing, the two girls were then the owners of the house and, as neither had qualified in medicine, I was not at all surprised when I received a delicate hint from Bryony that they wanted the place to themselves. For another thing, in a hive of gossip such as Abbots Crozier, I thought there might be – to put it mildly – remarks made about the relationship between a still youngish bachelor and two unmarried girls. Besides, Rant had always promised me a full partnership instead of the part-share which I had accepted when first I joined him, and in his will he left me enough money to buy my own practice.'

'Dr Mortlake, I want to hear about four deaths which have occurred, three of them over a fairly short period, the fourth recently. None of them appears to have been caused by old age or any terminal illness.'

'You don't mean – ?'

'It may come to that, in the final analysis, but I doubt it. I want those people cleared out of the way, that is all. I dislike unnecessary complications.'

'But, if I know the deaths to which you are referring, all four have been fully accounted for. There is no mystery about any of them.'

'You think not? A young and, so far as one knows, a healthy boy dies of septicaemia from a gash which, properly treated, should have caused no particular problem.'

'Oh, Dame Beatrice! You know what villagers are like. Three-quarters or more of them in Abbots Crozier have not even the basic notions of hygiene. The boy's aunt refused to have him attend Outpatients at the Axehead hospital and the lad agreed with her. In consequence, because of their negligence, the wound turned septic and that was that.'

'Not quite, surely? I understand that Dr Rant treated the wound.'

'Oh, look here!' said Mortlake uncomfortably. 'I can't criticise another doctor's treatment of his patient, even though that doctor is dead. You yourself are highly qualified in medicine. You know what the ethics of the profession entail.'

'I accept the implied rebuke, but your scruples need not extend further than you claim. What of Dr Rant as a family man; as a husband and father?'

The flush of anger and (Dame Beatrice guessed) embarrassment died away on Mortlake's fair-skinned cheeks. He looked troubled. He said at last that the couple had always behaved with the utmost correctness in his presence, but he had thought that their attitude towards one another in private might have been different. As for the two daughters, they had been in awe of their father, if not in actual fear of him. Bryony attempted to stand up to him now and again, but any sign of rebelliousness was soon nipped in the bud. She had gone to Mortlake himself after one inglorious set-to with her father and unburdened herself. All she had done, she said, was to beg her father to let her return to college so she could study to go on to university.

'Of course, Rant had flown off the handle,' said Mortlake. 'Mrs Rant had become a semi-invalid and he decided to end the girls' education and keep them at home to look after their mother and himself, and that's how it worked out. I was damned sorry for all of them, especially Bryony. She badly wanted to go to university and then get away from home and take a job.'

'Did Dr Rant have trouble in getting domestic help, then?' asked Laura.

'Well, what servants there were had to pluck up all their courage to give notice, I think, but, one by one, they did it and, in the end, not long before he died, he couldn't get any replacements. However much they needed a job, the village women fought shy of Crozier Lodge, especially after Mrs Rant died, so the two girls did everything.'

'I often wonder how Edward Moulton-Barrett managed to keep any servants,' said Laura. 'Didn't the girls resent being household drudges when their father, it seems, had so much money?'

'Bryony was deeply resentful; Morpeth is more malleable and so got most of the chores put on her. To be fair to Bryony, though, it must be allowed that she acted as her father's driver when he did his afternoon rounds, and so she was out of the house most afternoons.'

'Couldn't Dr Rant drive the car, then?' asked Laura.

'Oh, he did, until Bryony was old enough to handle it. After his wife's death, of course, it was better for his own and everybody else's safety that he did not drive.'

'I wonder he had any patients who still wanted him to visit them,' Laura observed. 'I'm dashed if *I* would have called him in.'

'Well, Mrs Gavin, you would have been surprised by Rant. I often was. After he had steeped himself at lunch, he was urbane, good-humoured, clear-headed and absolutely at his best. Of course, the reaction came later, usually after evening surgery, although quite often he would cry off the evening stint and leave me to cope with his patients as well as my own.'

'I also wonder,' said Laura bluntly, 'that you stayed with such a man.'

'Well,' said Mortlake apologetically, 'there was this promise to take me into equal partnership, you see.'

'You believed that a drunk like Rant would have kept his word?'

'I think the fact that he left me enough money to buy my own practice is proof, don't you?'

'Well, now,' said Dame Beatrice briskly, 'let us turn to the second of the deaths. An inquest was held, I am told, because the death was sudden and totally unexpected. What can you tell us about Mrs Subbock, Dr Mortlake?'

'I was doing the afternoon rounds when she met with her fatal accident. I attended the inquest, but was not called as a witness. There was nothing to which I could have testified.'

'But Dr Rant was called, I assume, and you heard his testimony.'

'Yes, and nobody could fault it. It was held at three in the afternoon because the coroner had been in the police court conducting a case for a client all the morning. Rant was – how shall I put it?'

'All tanked up?' suggested Laura.

'So, of course, he was at his best. We got the repercussions later. He said that he had seen Mrs Subbock to the door himself. She was so vituperative and abusive that he did not want either of his daughters or a servant to hear the bad language. He said he saw her on to the top of the front steps and then promptly shut the front door on her. Shortly afterwards, a man who had been working in the garden knocked on the door and said that the woman had fallen down the steps and that her head was bleeding and she had lost consciousness.'

'And the verdict was accidental death. What did you think of the verdict in Dr Rant's own case?'

'Oh, undoubtedly it was the correct one. The alternative could only have been suicide and nobody who knew Rant would have dreamed that he was capable of that.'

'Grief for the death of his wife, perhaps?'

'Oh, he missed her, of course, as a useful adjunct, but the drinking he did consoled him for his loss of one of the household serfs. He had plenty of money, work he could (and did) shove on to me when he didn't feel like doing it, and two grown-up daughters who had never shown any intention of getting married and who provided his meals and all his other domestic comforts. Rant was sitting far too pretty and was far too fond of himself and his bottle ever to have thought of suicide.'

'Interesting. But if he was so clear-headed in his cups, how do you account for his dangerous mixing of a drug he was taking and the alcohol to which he had become addicted?'

'The drug had soporific effects, I suppose. It must have muddled him to the extent that he forgot he had already taken the specified dose. Of course, he should have left the drinks alone at such a time, but he had lost the will to abstain and, again, the drug may have clouded his reasoning powers. I was called as a witness and I said all this. Nobody attempted to challenge the evidence I gave.'

'Were his drugs prescribed by you?' asked Laura.

'Good heavens, no! That would have been quite improper, as I was his assistant and living in his house. He prescribed for himself and Bryony or I was sent to the chemist's to pick up the bottles. The chemist is dead now, and the shop has been taken over by people who never knew Rant.'

Dame Beatrice asked no questions. She said, 'So we come to the fourth and most recent of the deaths in which I am interested, and not only I, but the police.'

'Oh, this chap who was found dead in the river? As a matter of fact, I'm interested in that. Three of us examined the body, you know, myself, a police doctor and then a pathologist from Lambridge. We agreed that, in all probability, the man, terrified of the dog he had tried to steal, had dashed into the river in an attempt to cross it and had slipped and cracked his skull and drowned while he was still unconscious.'

'Well, it appears that the police are not prepared to allow matters to rest on a verdict of accidental death. They have their suspicions. Has a man named Goodfellow ever consulted you?'

'Goodfellow? Not so far as I remember and I think one would remember a name like that. What is his first name?'

'Robin, or so he says.'

'Good Lord! Aren't parents odd when it comes to having their children christened! As for the corpse in the river, do you mean it was this Goodfellow chap?'

'I know it was not. The Rant sisters have met Goodfellow and they also saw the dead man. Goodfellow's was not the corpse in the river.'

'Strange that nobody has come forward.'

'The answer may be that the dead man was a foreigner. By that, I mean that he did really come from abroad. The villagers call everybody a foreigner who was not born in the place. This man, perhaps, was a chance visitor. Even so, if he was on holiday at one of the hotels or was staying at one of the cottages, one would think he would be missed and then his photograph recognised. How long did you and the police doctor think he had been dead?'

'One can't be precise when the body has been in water. The person who found him – this woman who works for the Rant sisters – had to get back to Crozier Lodge and on to the telephone, the police had to get from Axehead to Watersmeet, then the police doctor had to be summoned and he pulled me in to give a second opinion, as the circumstances were so unusual –'

'In what particular way?'

'Well, the dog was sitting on the trousers and the man was wearing nothing but briefs and a shirt. Anyway, we both came to the conclusion that he had been dead only a matter of a few hours.'

'At what time did you see him?'

'Between eleven and half-past.'

'If I suggested that he died at round about six o'clock, would that fit in with your findings?'

'Oh, yes, near enough.' The doctor looked interested. So far, Dame Beatrice thought, he had been slightly on the defensive, but not now. 'What do you know that I don't?' he asked brightly.

'Nothing which I can substantiate at present. Dr Mortlake, I would like to go back to the time of Dr Rant's death.'

'I can't tell you anything more about that. You have heard what I said in court. There is nothing more.'

'A question or two, if I may. You were living at Crozier Lodge at the time. You must have known what a foolish and dangerous course Dr Rant was pursuing by drinking heavily while he was taking a powerful drug. Did you never warn him?'

'Of course I did, but once and once only. He went for me with the bottle of gin he had just emptied. Luckily for me, he tripped on the edge of the rug and fell flat just before he reached me. I didn't approach the subject again after that. I decided it wasn't up to me to try to save his rotten life. I wondered whether it would be better if I left Crozier Lodge and washed my hands of him and his affairs, but I had nothing coming in at that time except the salary he paid me as his assistant – I will say for him that the money came regularly month by month because, when I first signed on, I insisted on having it paid by banker's order – but, apart from that, I felt that my presence in the house was a bit of protection for the two girls.'

'You were not in the least surprised when he died, I suppose, knowing what you did of his habits?'

Dr Mortlake hesitated. He fidgeted with the strap of his wristwatch so that he could look down and escape from the hypnotic effect of Dame Beatrice's brilliant black eyes. However, he was forced by her watchful silence to respond to her question.

'Well, to tell you the truth because it doesn't matter now, I had formed an opinion – not based, I hasten to add, on anything tangible, but just an opinion – that although he had taken my warning so badly, he had begun to heed it.'

'So you *were* surprised when he died.'

'Oh, well, not really. The alcohol alone would have done for him in the end. He died a bit *sooner* than I expected, that is all.'

'Was the nature of the drug he was taking revealed at the inquest?'

'Well, the chemist was called and a very scared man he was. He could not produce the prescription. He said that Dr Rant was hoping to patent the production and get a multiple firm of chemists to promote it, so he insisted that each prescription should be destroyed when the drug was collected. The chemist testified that the contents varied a little from time to time, as Dr Rant (he supposed) continued his experiments. The coroner did not press the man, as, of course, he ought to have done, and I myself have no idea what the mixture was, since the bottles were always most carefully washed out as soon as they were empty.'

'That chap is a smooth talker,' said Laura later.

'The bedside manner, perhaps,' said Dame Beatrice, 'but what he told us was revealing, I thought, didn't you?'

10

Dead in the Valley

'I think you ought to have a lock put on that door,' said Susan one day to Bryony. 'Now that you've heard one tramp has used the loft as a doss-house, others may follow and some may be very rough types. Besides, it's known all over the place that you two are alone here at night. You ought to make the front gates secure as well. You can always let me have a key.'

'Something in what Susan says, don't you think?' said Morpeth to her sister when the kennel-maid had gone out with two of the hounds. 'I don't at all care for the thought of a tramp getting into the grounds and sleeping in the loft. After all, if people know we are alone I expect they also know that, except for harmless, goofy old Sekhmet, the hounds are shut away at night and can't protect us.'

'I agree. We'll have a padlock put on the front gates and another on the outside of the loft door. Well, shopping day, so I'll get the padlocks in Axehead while I'm doing the rest of it.'

'Why don't you teach *me* to drive the car? We could then take it in turn to do the shopping.'

'You're too nervous to make a good driver. Besides, I don't think you would ever pass the test.'

'We don't know that until I've tried.'

'This is no part of the country for a learner-driver. It takes me all my time to negotiate the road down to Abbots Bay and the hill to Axehead. I'll teach you the rudiments out on the moor, if you like. It's quiet and safe up there, but it wouldn't help you at all when you face sharp bends and traffic and a hill of one in four when you wanted to get into Axehead.'

Morpeth said no more. She was not at all anxious to have the responsibility of driving the car, and the realisation that a driving test would have to be taken daunted her. When her sister had gone shopping, she prepared the vegetables for lunch and played for a time with Sekhmet and a rubber ball. It then occurred to her that a tramp, even though Adams had described him to her as 'summat a cut above the usual', might have left the loft very untidy and possibly in an offensive condition which ought to be dealt with before the door was padlocked against further intruders.

Morpeth armed herself with dustpan, soft-haired brush and a duster and walked over to the garage. She mounted the outside stair and opened the door of the loft. The room had a window, but she left the door wide open in order to obtain more light as she looked around her.

The room appeared to be in order. She saw her father's old but favourite armchair, a table with some books on it, his desk with its drawers and a wardrobe from which she and Bryony had taken his clothes. They had disposed of them to a church jumble sale in Axehead except for his raincoat and a tweed hat he put on when he went fishing. Both garments were too grubby to be offered in such a state and Bryony had decided that it was not worth the money to have them cleaned.

There seemed nothing much which needed to be done in tidying the room except to dust it. Morpeth did this thoroughly, shaking the duster out at the open doorway every now and then. She opened the drawers, but they were empty, as she expected. It occurred to her that she ought to inspect the interior of the wardrobe in case the intruder had used it as a convenience. Dreading that such might be the case, she hesitated for a bit and then nerved herself to make the inspection.

The wardrobe was empty. The bag which the doctor had carried with him on his afternoon calls on his patients, the ancient raincoat and the hat which Morpeth knew had been left in the wardrobe had gone. Morpeth, although fearing it was useless, searched the room again. Then she left the loft and went back to the house. On Bryony's return from shopping, they unpacked the baskets, put away the food and the other household necessities, and made coffee. When they had settled down, Morpeth broke the news of the disappearance of the hat, bag and raincoat.

'Father's bag gone, and that old raincoat and hat?' said Bryony. 'Must have been taken by the tramp Adams talked about. I suppose the man thought he could sell them, especially the leather bag. Is anything else missing?'

'Not so far as I know. Perhaps you would go and have a look round. You see, if the bag is missing, father's scalpels and perhaps other dangerous things have gone. The bag was fitted up just as he left it.'

'After lunch, then. There's no hurry. Have you done the vegetables? Susan will enjoy the cutlets I've brought in. What's she doing this morning?'

'She is still out. She must be taking Anubis and Amon for a longer walk than usual.'

Susan came back with startling and disturbing news.

'Police all over the moor,' she said. 'A hiker has found a body in that rocky valley which runs out to Castercombe.'

'Not another dead body?' exclaimed Bryony.

'Yes, I'm afraid so. I met the shepherd whose flock graze the pastures below Cowlass Hill and he says the man's throat was cut.'

'How horrible! Worse than the other death! At least that one was brought in as accident. This one must have been murder or suicide,' said Bryony.

'Yes, I suppose so. What's for lunch?'

'You feel like having lunch after hearing a thing like that?' asked Morpeth.

'I didn't see the body and I'm hungry.'

'Did the police stop you?'

'No. I was right over near the Witch's Cauldron rock and they were mostly on the road. I thought they might be looking for somebody who had escaped from Castercombe gaol. Then,

when I got to Cowlass Hill and met the shepherd, he told me
what had happened. He got the low-down from his son, who
happens to be a policeman. It seems to be a suicide so I suppose it was all right for the policeman to blab.'

'Did you see the police on your way back?'

'No. I kept well in the shelter of the rocks and then I took
the cliff path, which is quite hidden from the road. Anyway, I
think they were too busy to notice me.'

'You were determined to dodge them, I suppose,' said
Bryony. 'Well, I don't blame you.'

'I should think not indeed!' said Susan, her sun-and-wind-
roughed face flushing angrily. 'If you had been given the
going-over they gave me when they were in my cottage and
found that silly hat and the piece of trouser-band, you would
have dodged them, too. It was my rotten luck to find that dead
man at Watersmeet and I don't want any more to do with dead
bodies for a long time to come, thank you!'

The news was all over the village by the early evening. The
three women had supper at seven and Susan, presumably on
her way home, called at the Crozier Arms for a beer and then,
to the surprise of the sisters, she came back to Crozier Lodge
with as much of the matter as she had been able to gather at
the pub.

'Didn't like to ask any questions,' she said, 'me not being
exactly what you might call popular in the village, but the
barmaid was getting a pretty lurid account from a man who
had a cousin in the telephone exchange in Axehead, so I
gathered an earful, but whether it was fact or romance I
wouldn't care to guess. Apparently the police plan to telephone the hotels to find out whether any guest is missing, as
nobody in the village seems to know anything.'

'Well, it doesn't sound like a convict, does it? Where was
the body found?' asked Bryony.

'I told you, near enough. I don't know the exact spot.'

'Perhaps the poor man had a sudden fit of depression. That

valley can be very lonely at times and it's a nasty spooky place, anyway,' said Morpeth. 'Some people think it's haunted.'

'Talking of lonely and spooky,' said Susan, 'would you mind if I kippd here for the night? That's what I came back to ask.'

'It's not like you to be nervous,' said Bryony, 'but stay by all means, if you want to. I wonder how soon the police will know who the dead man was?'

'Goodness knows. I suppose they'll put out photographs, as they did of the man I found. This village will be getting itself a bad name if any more people die on holiday here.'

Nobody came forward to identify the dead man, so the police did as Susan had predicted. A day or two after Susan had returned to Crozier Lodge to make her report, Morpeth recognised a picture in the local paper. The sisters had gone into Axehead to take Nephthys to the vet for a check-up, as the hound had begun to scratch an ear and seemed slightly off her food. Morpeth had to pass a newsagent's after she had left Bryony sitting in the car in the carpark, so she went into the shop to buy a couple of women's magazines which the sisters favoured and which they passed on to Susan when they had finished with them.

A small pile of the papers was lying on the counter, so that Morpeth could not help seeing them. Feeling a sense of shock, since the caption above the picture on the front page was eye-catching and in large print, she picked up a paper, bought it and the magazines, and went on to the veterinary surgery with a sense of foreboding and deep unease, for she had no doubt whatever that the newspaper picture was that of Goodfellow. It was not the photograph of a dead man. It was that of an artist's impression of what Goodfellow would have looked like before his throat was severed, but Morpeth had no difficulty in recognising the face.

In the vet's waiting-room she realised this with a sick feeling of horror mixed with resentment at the tricks Fate seemed to be playing. The half-dozen other pet-owners, having looked up, but without curiosity, when she entered, returned to their magazines or to stroking their cats, and paid her no further attention. Her excitement made her impatient of delay. She felt that she could not return quickly enough to the carpark to show Bryony the newspaper.

Half an hour's waiting-time before Nephthys could receive attention caused her to calm down and reflect upon what her next move should be. Obviously it was her duty to report to the police that she knew something important about the dead man and, for what it was worth, could give his name. In her naive, almost childish way, she thought the police would be sufficiently grateful for the information to give up pestering Susan and themselves about the body found in the river. Instead, therefore, of taking the hound straight back to the car park, she called at the Axehead police station. An enlarged copy of the newspaper picture was conspicuously displayed at the side of the front door. Morpeth looked at it, hitched the hound's lead to the railings and said, 'Good girl, stay!'

'You'd better see the Chief, miss,' said the desk sergeant resignedly, when she had stated the purpose of her visit. 'Yours is the sixth story, up to date. They range from telling us the man was an oil baron to suggesting he was the victim of a secret society, so I hope your account will seem a bit more sensible. You say you knew the man?'

'Well, I had met him. He called on us, thinking one of us was a doctor. He was quite insane, you know. I'm not a bit surprised he committed suicide.'

'Come this way, miss.' Morpeth and the detective-inspector had met at Crozier Lodge over the former enquiry. Harrow greeted her in avuncular fashion as soon as the sergeant showed her in.

'Well, well, well!' he said. 'Sit down, won't you, Miss Rant? So you've come along to help us.'

'I don't know how much help it will be,' said Morpeth, 'because I'm not at all sure that the name he gave us was his real name. He was quite mad, you see.'

'So what name did he give you?'

'He called himself Robin Goodfellow, but he also told us that he was Ozymandias, king of kings. When we heard that, Bryony thought he was a case for a psychiatrist and the only one we knew was Dame Beatrice, so Bryony took him to the Stone House.'

'That would be Dame Beatrice Lestrange Bradley, of course. I'll have a word with her. Now, to another point, Miss Rant: the woman who acts as your kennel-maid found the body of that man in the river, didn't she? We understand that on the morning of this Goodfellow's death – if you are right and the dead man *is* the man you knew – she was out on the moor with a couple of your dogs. She met a shepherd over Cowlass Hill way, didn't she?'

'We always take the hounds on to the moor for a run. There's nothing in that. Susan would naturally go there.'

'Did she often go as far as the lower slopes of Cowlass Hill?'

'I don't know. We please ourselves how long we stay out and how far we go. It mostly depends on the weather.'

'She did meet this shepherd out there, though, didn't she?'

'Yes, she said so. She made no bones about telling us,' said Morpeth, beginning to panic. 'How do you know it was Susan? She wouldn't have given the shepherd her name, meeting him casually like that.'

'We have our methods.' He was careful not to add that the police had not known for certain, until that moment, which woman the shepherd had spoken with. The shepherd had proved very inept at describing a female whom he had never previously met, but he had described the Pharaoh hounds this woman was exercising, so it was merely a case of finding out which of the three from Crozier Lodge had been out on the moor that morning. Harrow felt a sense of triumph now that he knew Susan had been the one. Almost too good to be true, he thought, but it *was* true. She had found the first body, incriminating evidence had been discovered at her cottage, and now it was clear that she had been in the vicinity of a second man on the morning of his death.

Harrow was still in the dark as to the reason for Susan's having left her cottage so early on the morning of the Watersmeet death. He had made attempts to get her to change her story, but she adhered to her assertion that she had been for a swim, although he had made it very clear that he did not believe her.

'Look,' said Morpeth desperately, 'if the man was found in Rocky Valley and Susan met the shepherd near the foot of Cowlass Hill, she wouldn't have known anything about what had happened until the shepherd told her. There is more than one way of getting to that hill.'

'The valley opens out on to those hill pastures, and most people go that way, Miss Rant.'

'But you can take the cliff path to Castercombe and bypass the valley altogether.'

'You did *what*?' said Bryony, when Morpeth got back to the carpark and showed her sister the newspaper picture. 'Well, you *have* put your foot in it! Poor old Susan!'

'Susan wouldn't have known who the dead man was, even if she had passed beside the corpse. She was out with Isis and Nephthys when Goodfellow called on us and he never came near us again after you had taken him to see Dame Beatrice. We can both swear that Susan had never set eyes on him and wouldn't have a clue to who he was.'

'I'm going to ask whether we can call at the Stone House this afternoon. I think Dame Beatrice ought to know about this.'

'I expect she does know. It's in the papers.'

The detective-inspector had got there first. Polly, the maid who answered the door, informed the sisters that Dame Beatrice and Mrs Gavin had two policemen with them. 'But come in, miss, do,' she said to Bryony. 'The ladies won't be long, if you'd care to wait. They're in the library.' She showed Bryony and Morpeth into the drawing-room. 'I don't suppose they'll be all that long,' she repeated comfortingly. 'The police hasn't much time to waste, nor have our two ladies. You can play the piano if you want. They'll not hear it from here.'

Bryony had preserved a long silence which had lasted for the whole of the journey. When the door had closed behind Polly, she broke into speech.

'So the police have beaten us to it,' she said. 'I can't think what made you go to the police station before you had spoken to me about that wretched newspaper picture.'

'I did what I thought was the best.'

'The way to hell – ! Oh, well, it's done now. I wish, all the same, that we'd got our story to Dame Beatrice before the police arrived.'

'I don't see what difference it makes.'

'Of course it makes a difference.' She lapsed into a brooding silence again. Morpeth stood it for the next ten minutes and then she went over to the piano and began very softly to strum. This did nothing to relieve the tension. 'Oh, for heaven's sake!' Bryony exclaimed. Fortunately, soon after this Laura came into the room.

'Sorry we had to park you,' she said. 'The rozzers have gone, so I'll ring for tea and then you can tell us why you've come.'

'I suppose,' said Bryony bluntly, when tea had been brought and Dame Beatrice had joined them, 'it's no good asking what was said between you and the detectives?'

Dame Beatrice cackled and replied that she saw no need for absolute secrecy. She proceeded to give an account of the interview. It had begun when she was asked whether it was true that she had been called upon to treat a patient named Robin Goodfellow.

'Well,' said Morpeth, as she and her sister drove home, 'I hope you are not going to continue the great silence. You know how I hate it when you don't speak to me.'

'I'm sorry I was angry with you. Perhaps, after all, you did the right thing in going straight to the police when you saw that madman's picture in the newspaper.'

'Dame Beatrice told them that in her opinion – and she

made it in her professional capacity – he was not a madman.'

'I don't have to agree. Only a madman would cut his own throat.'

'People do that sort of thing in a fit of depression, not because they're mad.'

'I didn't notice that Goodfellow gave us any impression of feeling depressed when we met him, nor in the car when I took him to the Stone House.'

Back in that Georgian domicile, Dame Beatrice and Laura were conducting their own conversation.

'You told them you saw no need for secrecy,' said Laura, 'but you withheld the most important point, didn't you?'

'I thought I qualified it by saying ''absolute'' secrecy. Are you thinking of anything in particular?'

'You didn't mention that the police think the throat-slitting was not suicide but murder.'

'My dear Laura, that word was never mentioned. I am aware of what the police think, but they were careful not to say it.'

'And you were careful not to put the word into their mouths.'

'All they said was that they had not found the implement with which the deed was done.'

'Well, wasn't that tantamount to saying the man had been murdered? You can't cut your throat and then get rid of the knife or whatever it was.'

'The part of the valley where the hiker found the body is no longer cordoned off, we were told. I think that tomorrow we will drive over there and look at –'

'The spot marked with a cross?'

'The police were not sufficiently informative to make certain that we can do that, but I would like to obtain a general view of the setting.'

'Fancy Morpeth's having the guts to take action without first consulting Bryony!'

'You mean that, on her own initiative, she went to the police? It was an impulse she may live to regret.'

'Why?'

'I do not like this disappearance of the coat, hat and bag from that loft.'

'There doesn't seem much doubt about who had those. The poacher Adams knew of that room, so did the tramp he found asleep there, so, possibly, did the prowler they talked about and, if one tramp, why not others? It would get around that the Rants are on their own at night and that there is no lock on the front gates – and none, so far, on the door to the loft. All these points have come out in conversation at various times and, I thought, were emphasised today.'

'Yes,' agreed Dame Beatrice, 'but there is one point which you appear to have overlooked. There are three other people, in addition to those you have listed, who knew what the loft contained.'

'Four,' said Laura. 'I suppose Dr Mortlake would have known. He lived in the house long enough and didn't move out until after Dr Rant's death. He doesn't seem to have left until the will was proved and he knew he could go into practice on his own. He may even have helped the Rants to clear up their father's things and get rid of his clothes. The doctor's bag is missing, Morpeth told us. Who would want it except another doctor? Mortlake, beware! "There's a porpoise close behind you and he's treading on your tail!" Oh, I'm not serious,' Laura added hastily as she caught Dame Beatrice's eye.

' "Dare to be a Daniel," ' responded Dame Beatrice. ' "Dare to stand alone, dare to have a *porpoise* firm and dare to make it known!" Your powers of imagination have rendered me, as usual, faint but pursuing. Dr Mortlake? You open up strange and terrifying vistas.'

Laura spread out shapely hands and opened up another vista, or thought she did.

'If they would let you see the body,' she said, 'could you tell whether the throat had been cut with a doctor's scalpel?'

'I am not a forensic expert and I have no intention of asking to see the body,' Dame Beatrice replied.

'Throat-cutting must be a very messy business. Wouldn't

the murderer have got smothered in blood?'

'Perhaps not if, as the police seem to think, the victim was seized by the hair from behind, his head pulled back and one swift and deadly slash made across his throat.'

'With a scalpel?' persisted Laura.

'The police did not offer a suggestion as to the nature of the weapon, as you know. They merely said that they had not found anything with which the lethal wound could have been inflicted.'

'Perhaps the hiker who found the body spotted a knife and pocketed it. Seems unlikely. Oh, well, they say all murderers make at least one mistake. What interests me is the fate of the doctor's bag. Bryony told us that the three scalpels Dr Rant possessed were rolled up in a soft leather hold-all rather like some manicure sets people take when they're travelling. Where do you think the doctor's old waterproof and his tweed hat have gone? Morpeth says she found them missing when she went to clear up that loft. Did they go at the same time as the bag, I wonder?'

'I am going on the assumption that the person the poacher saw talking to the tramp outside Sekhmet's kennel that morning was wearing them, but no mention was made of a bag, so I may be mistaken. However, Adams' somewhat inadequate description of the clothes the person was wearing coincides quite interestingly with Morpeth's account of the missing rain-coat and hat.'

'You say "person". I notice that you don't commit yourself as to sex.'

'The poacher himself admitted that he was unable to guess whether the stranger was a man or a woman,' said Dame Beatrice. 'I wonder what light the inquest will throw on this second unnatural death?'

'Yes, Abbots Crozier is fast becoming a hissing and a byword for a danger spot. As for the inquest, perhaps it will tell us whether Robin Goodfellow was the man's real name. My own view is that it was as much of an *alias* as Ozymandias.

Still, parents have the weirdest flights of fancy when it comes
to naming their children, as poor Morpeth Rant knows to her
cost. Fancy naming a baby after a folk dance!'

'Morpeth is as pleasant a name as Elspeth,' remarked Dame
Beatrice, 'if it is taken on its own. As for the inquest, well, I
have no wish to seem ghoulish, but I am looking forward to it.'

The death at Watersmeet had attracted very little attention
outside the immediate neighbourhood of Axehead, Abbots
Bay and Abbots Crozier and would hardly have merited more
than a few lines in the local paper had it not been for the
bizarre incident of Sekhmet and the dead man's trousers.
Unless or until they could prove their theory that the man had
been murdered and his trousers stripped off him and given to
the dog before the body had been put into the river, the police
were keeping very quiet about the whole Watersmeet affair.

The valley murder, as it came to be called, was a very different
matter. The big dailies ran it as front-page news and the *London
Postmark* devoted its double centre page to a set of photographs
of the area. Broadcasts and television coverage followed, and
Abbots Bay and Abbots Crozier, together with Axehead, where
the inquest was opened, swarmed with reporters and camera-
men. Accommodation in both the villages and the town was
stretched to its limits and there was even an overflow into
Castercombe.

The medical evidence indicated that the victim had been
attacked from behind and his head pulled back. One slash had
severed the jugular vein. The identification of the body posed
a problem for the police because it threw more open the vexing
business of discovering who the murderer was.

The corpse was identified by a smart London policeman
neither as Ozymandias nor Robin Goodfellow, although the
man had been known for some time under the latter name. He
turned out to be a very shady private eye known also to the
Metropolitan Police as Hillingdon. The media had done their
work and the pictures of the dead man had been compared

with those in police files, for Ozymandias had done time for larceny. The inquest was then adjourned pending further police enquiries and the search for the weapon responsible for Hillingdon's death.

'I think,' said Dame Beatrice, 'that this murder ties up with the death at Watersmeet.'

This opinion was endorsed by Detective-Inspector Harrow to his sergeant.

'Ten to one,' he said, 'this Hillingdon, as we've now got to call him, knew something about that Watersmeet business, and died because of what he knew.'

'So if we knew who the Watersmeet killer was – and we're still convinced that was murder, not accident – we could spot the valley murderer, sir.'

'All sorts of trouble about that, the way I see it. As there's a London end to this business, we could be looking for a needle in a haystack unless the Metropolitan Police come in and help. If only we could get a clear identification of that Watersmeet corpse it might help.'

'The two deaths were, of course, quite unlike. Murderers usually repeat their effects.'

'Oh, well, we must just soldier on with this Rocky Valley business. That place has got itself a bad name locally. It's a queer sort of landscape and not a bit like anywhere else in that neighbourhood.'

'According to what I've heard, sir, nobody goes that way after sunset if they're cycling or on foot, and motorists prefer the coast road, although it's the longer way to Castercombe from Axehead.'

'Nobody goes that way after sunset? Makes it an ideal place for a murder, doesn't it? According to the doctors, death had occurred the night before the body was found. The two men must have met by arrangement and both wanted the transaction kept secret, I reckon.'

'Brings us back to the Watersmeet business. According to Adams, two men or a man and a woman met in the Rants'

garden before the household was stirring. It is more than possible that the man found dead in the river later in the day was
one of them.'

'Sounds like people who knew the Rants' garden *and* the
valley, doesn't it? – or, anyway, one of them did.'

'And knew that Watersmeet would most likely be deserted
so early in the morning. It sounds like three assignations: one
in the Rants' garden, one at Watersmeet, and this one in
Rocky Valley – and the last two with unsuspecting victims.
What do you think about one of the Rant sisters? We are
already keeping an eye on that dog-woman of theirs. All three
women are out every day with those hounds and must know
the countryside like the backs of their hands.'

11

Scalpels

The valley indeed had a sinister reputation. Robin Goodfellow was not the first to have met with a violent death there. At one time the distance between Castercombe and Axehead, then a flourishing port, could be covered only on foot or on horseback, since no coach could cope with the descent or ascent from what became the village of Abbots Crozier after Abbots Bay needed to expand.

There was a coast road between Castercombe and Axehead, but the journey was a long one, and during the old coaching days before the sea wall was heightened and improved the thoroughfare was often under water. The valley was sheltered and the road through it was always passable, although the surface was very rough and travellers carried weapons. But, even in those times, nobody risked the valley after dark for there were stories of attacks, some of them fatal, by highway bands who emerged suddenly from behind the jagged and fantastically shaped outcroppings of rock. It was commonly held that there were ghostly as well as human agencies to be feared.

One exception had been a party of amateur ghost-hunters, but, although they were reticent about their experiences, most of them declared that they would not care to brave the valley again after nightfall.

At Hallowe'en and at other times which were kept secret, the local witches held a meeting in the valley and fearful happenings ensued.

However, it was far from dark when, on the morning following the visit of the police and the sisters Rant to the Stone House, Dame Beatrice and Laura, having booked lunch at the Headlands hotel, drove westwards towards Cowlass Hill and Castercombe.

'Well,' said Laura, 'from what little we were told, it doesn't seem that Goodfellow was killed all that far from the village. Hullo! We are not the only seekers after truth, it seems.'

Three police cars were parked off the road and not far from them were a couple of caravans and some tents. Uniformed policemen and what appeared to be a troop of Guides were searching the heather and beating down the bracken. Directing operations was a police inspector, also in uniform. The police were in shirt-sleeves, for the day was already warming up.

Laura parked the car just off the road and she and Dame Beatrice got out. A little knot of idlers, probably holiday-makers, was watching the scene from the roadside. Laura and Dame Beatrice joined them. The inspector came up.

'Nobody to leave the roadside,' he said.

'Then what are the Guides doing among the local vegetation?' asked Laura.

Before the inspector could reply, Dame Beatrice presented her official card. His authoritative attitude changed. Having been introduced to Laura, he led them away from the sight-seers and said, 'My apologies, madam. Only trying to keep the general public off our pitch, although what they think they're going to see, goodness knows.' He turned to Laura. 'The Girl Guides are helping us,' he said. 'They stick at a dull job better than boys do, and don't go skylarking about. They had per-mission to camp here, so we thought we'd make them useful.'

'They were not camping here at the time of the incident, of course?' said Dame Beatrice.

'Came from Bristol about an hour ago. They're helping us look for the murder weapon, although we don't call it that. I don't think anything will turn up. If the murderer has any sense, he'll have taken the weapon away with him and dis-posed of it elsewhere.'

'Were the caravans here when it happened?' asked Laura.

'No, Mrs Gavin, they are ours. We're keeping a round-the-clock watch on this part of the valley in case anything emerges.'

'Including the murderer?'

'Well, you never know.'

'I wonder the Guide leader likes the idea of having a camp so near the scene of a pretty horrible crime.'

'The young lady didn't know about it until I took her aside and told her. Anyway, we are moving them on this afternoon. Found them a much better site in a farmer's field at the foot of Cowlass Hill. When they turned up here, I thought it better to let them into the area and make themselves useful, especially as we no longer needed to cordon off the area once the body had been photographed and removed.'

'Well,' said Laura to Dame Beatrice, as they walked back to the car, 'at least we know where it happened.'

'And, thanks to the courtesy of the police force, we know when. Susan, according to what the Rant sisters told us yesterday, appeared to think that the death had occurred on the morning when she had the news from the shepherd, but Goodfellow had been dead for at least twelve hours when the police doctor examined him.'

'You know, it's the wrong way about.'

'How so?'

'Well, if a crackpot like Ozymandias had slit somebody's throat, I wouldn't be surprised, but that Mr Oz himself should be the victim does surprise me.'

'To begin with, Goodfellow was not what you call a crackpot. To continue, he was carrying out a masquerade which may have threatened danger to someone. I think he must have had an assignation here with his murderer.'

'But why choose a place like this valley?'

'Nobody in this neighbourhood recognised the picture in the newspaper until Morpeth saw it. That indicates that Goodfellow was not resident in these parts unless he was in hiding hereabouts. He must have bought food for himself, but he could not have shopped in either of the villages or in Axehead; or someone besides Morpeth would probably have come forward with what they knew of him.'

Dame Beatrice had booked rooms for herself and Laura at the Headlands hotel. As they drove back to it for lunch, Laura asked the reason for their stay. It appeared that Dame Beatrice wished to keep in close touch with Bryony and Morpeth, that she was interested in Susan, and that she felt a personal interest in Goodfellow.

'And now,' said Laura, 'what's the *real* reason?' Dame Beatrice cackled, but did not reply directly. Her only response was to remark, as they turned into the hotel carpark, that lunch was served from one o'clock onwards and that Laura might like a walk in order to work up an appetite for it.

Laura was pleased with this suggestion. She saw her employer established in the small garden overlooking the sea four hundred feet below, brought her a glass of sherry and promised to be back in about an hour. The hotel was not far from the top of the cliff railway and her first thought was to go down into Abbots Bay and explore the village. When she reached the little terminus, however, she changed her mind. There was a narrow lane leading away from the cliffs to her left. She calculated that it would take her to the valley again, with its fascinating rock formations and its brooding air of mystery and evil.

She chose this route, therefore, and, where the short, steeply sloping lane turned westwards, she found herself on a cliff path with the high bank of the hill on one side and a long drop to the sea on the other. The path was about four feet wide and it followed the shape of the hill. It was obviously man-made and fairly recent; it had been constructed, Laura supposed, for the benefit of the summer visitors.

Unlike the valley, in which the rocks made deep pools of shadow, the path, all along, was in full sunshine. There were gulls, the sea was glittering with silver, and on the landward bank there were the slender-flowered thistle, the rest-harrow, low-growing gorse and even, Laura discovered, the upright clover, an exile from Cornwall or Jersey. There was also a wood vetch, no stranger to rocky cliffs, which had attached its tendrils to a small bush of hawthorn.

She did not hurry. Now and again she met holidaymakers or was overtaken by them, but they were few. At a bend in the path there was a bit of flat rock which offered a seat. She accepted the invitation and gazed out to sea, then let her eyes rest on a big patch of thrift which was growing a few feet down the cliff. Near it was a tangle of brambles and caught up in the brambles was a brown object which was certainly not a paper bag tossed away by some litter-lout.

Laura looked at this object until curiosity got the better of her. The cliff was not precipitous at this point, and she was tall, with long arms. There was nobody else about, so she spreadeagled herself on the short, dry grass and stretched downwards. She could not reach the object, so she hoisted herself forward and tried again, this time with success.

Wriggling her way backwards from the edge of the cliff, she returned to the stone seat to examine her find. It was a roll of soft leather fastened by a narrow strap of the same material. Laura unfastened the strap and unrolled the little hold-all. Its contents were three scalpels – all, so far as she could see, clean and polished. The blades were less than two inches long and their shapes differed from one another according to the function each was designed to perform.

Conscious that her find might be of importance to the police, she looked with some excitement at the scalpels, but did not touch them. She rolled up the little bundle, fastened the strap, dropped the prize into the case from which she had removed her binoculars, slung the binoculars, separately from their case, by their own safety strap, around her neck, got up and decided to return at once to the hotel. She was hardly on her feet, however, when round the bend came two sand-coloured hounds followed by Morpeth Rant. They were heading towards the village, apparently on their way home.

Laura walked towards them, greetings were exchanged and Morpeth asked what Laura was doing in the neighbourhood. 'Have you heard any more about Ozymandias?' she enquired. 'It was I who recognised the picture in the paper, you know.'

'Dame Beatrice is interested in the police search for the murder weapon. We're staying tonight at the Headlands.'

'You would think his friends would have come forward by this time, wouldn't you? Oh, well, I had better be getting back. There are the runner beans to do for lunch. Bryony is so wasteful when she strings them that I don't like leaving them to her.'

'Where does this path bring me out?' asked Laura, who had changed her mind about going straight back to the hotel with what she had retrieved from the cliff.

'Oh, into the valley and about halfway along it. You may meet Susan. She is walking Isis and Nephthys, but I expect they are out on the open moor, so you may not see them if you are going back to the hotel when you reach the valley.'

They parted, and Morpeth appeared to have taken it for granted that Laura would be continuing her walk; for she made no suggestion that they should go together as far as the cliff railway. In any case, Laura was not in the mood for Morpeth's or anybody else's company. She wondered, but only idly, why Morpeth had chosen to take the cliff path. It was not the ideal location in which to exercise fairly large and extremely active dogs, for it was a favourite walk for visitors. Laura glanced at her watch and began to stride out. The binoculars' case now contained the leather bundle and the binoculars bounced against her chest on their short strap, so she unhitched the longer strap, that which was attached to the leather case, and swung it from her hand.

The cliff path ended with a view of the most spectacular outcrop in the valley. It was the Witch's Cauldron, and from where she stood, Laura thought she could see why it had been given that name. Between two crags, cut as clear as stencils against the morning sky, the blue gap looked like a hag with a sharply pointed profile wearing voluminous skirts.

As Laura walked on, the figure vanished and the rock presented the appearance of battlements. Below her, there was an area of grass, an oasis in a wilderness of rocks, bracken and heather which, from the evidence of a carefully mown patch in the middle of it, appeared to be the local cricket pitch.

Laura descended into the valley by a steep, rough path and found, on her right, a slope of grass which formed a kind of amphitheatre for cricket spectators. Whether the grass was natural or had been lovingly provided by the devotees of a game once played in gentlemanly and sporting fashion without the aid of bouncers, facemasks and illogical appeals for l.b.w., Laura did not know. The cricket ground was a small one, all that could be conjured out of that otherwise inhospitable and arid valley, but it was a tiny miracle in such a setting.

Above it, opposite Laura, was a fortress of rock pinnacles, and below her was the stony road traversing the valley.

Descending to it, she set a brisk pace towards the village, but when she came to the place where the hiker had found the murdered body, she slowed down. The caravans and the Guides' tents had gone, but the signs of police-trampled grass and bracken still marked the spot.

Laura did not come to a halt. There was a knot of sightseers who had heard the news of the murder and she had no intention of joining them. She swung the strap which held the camera case and its contents and got into her stride again.

There was time for a drink before lunch. She had it in the hotel bar, went to her room to change her shoes and then joined Dame Beatrice in the garden.

The afternoon was a busy one. Having been shown the scalpels in their leather case – this in the privacy of Laura's bedroom – Dame Beatrice decided to take the bundle immediately to the police station and hand it over.

'The things all look clean enough,' said Laura.

'A stream runs through the valley, I noticed,' said Dame

Beatrice, 'and I have no doubt the crime was premeditated and that the murderer had come with materials to clean the weapon. However, present-day methods of testing for blood-stains are well advanced and if there is the slightest trace of them the forensic experts will find it.'

The detective-inspector accompanied them up to Abbots Crozier and, while Dame Beatrice remained in the hotel, Laura guided him to the spot at which she had seen the little leather case. He asked whether she could be certain, so she indicated the flat outcrop upon which she had seated herself and directed his attention to the clump of beautiful pink thrift and the tangle of bramble runners.

'Careless of the chap,' he said. 'Anybody could have spotted it if they had happened to take a seat on that ledge, as you did. Why on earth didn't he chuck it further down the cliff where nobody could have seen it either from above or below?'

'I think he thought he had,' said Laura. 'If he and the murdered man had arranged to meet in the valley when no holidaymakers were about, it must have been almost dark. I imagine the murderer was in a great hurry to get back to wher-ever he had come from and chose this cliff path so as not to go into Abbots Crozier past any of the cottages. From the top of the cliff railway it's no distance to the zigzag path down to Abbots Bay. Goodness knows where he went from there.'

'So you think that the murder was committed in the semi-darkness, so it might have been quite dark before he had cleaned up and taken to the cliff path?'

'Yes, and thought he had thrown the leather case safely away.'

'Of course,' said the detective-inspector, 'there's no proof yet that a scalpel was the murder weapon, you know. There is no doubt the case was stolen from that loft, but the thief may have decided that what he had stolen might identify him if he tried to sell it. He may not have known what the scalpels were, but I suppose he realised they were no ordinary implements. I wouldn't be at all surprised if he chucked away *all* the contents of the doctor's bag and simply sold the bag itself. I must find out from the Rant daughters whether their father's initials were on the bag.'

'The bag won't matter all that much if one of the scalpels was not the murder weapon,' said Laura.

'Ah, well, we shall know more about that when Forensic have had their go, Mrs Gavin.' His sergeant, who had remained in the police car which had brought him to Abbots Crozier, departed with him and Laura rejoined Dame Beatrice and asked what came next on the agenda. Dame Beatrice replied that a visit to the Rants, the real reason for their stay in Abbots Crozier, was the next item.

'There are some questions I want to put to them and to Susan,' she said. 'Now that we have had this second death, a pattern begins to emerge.'

'As how? One took place soon after dawn at Watersmeet and was a drowning following severe concussion; the other must have happened at dusk in Rocky Valley and was caused by a throat-slitting. There is still a doubt, even, as to whether the first death was a murder at all, but there is certainly no doubt about the second one. I don't see much of a pattern emerging. The only thing common to both is that Susan seems to have been involved in some way. She found the first body and was told about the second one.'

'Your comments are very just. Do you think it rather more than coincidence that two unnatural deaths have occurred within such a short period of time so near a village as small as Abbots Crozier?'

'Well, there are all these holiday visitors around and about. Apparently, one of them found the second body. Who is to say that he himself wasn't the murderer of Ozymandias? Do you think I might ring up Axehead and ask what they know about the chap? After all, they owe me something for finding the scalpels for them.'

'True, but if you had not found them, I think somebody

else would have done so and might have thought it necessary to hand them over to the police.'

'Somebody who knew what they were and that a doctor had lost them? Yes, I suppose that's more than likely. The case has already had a fair amount of coverage in the press, so anybody who found anything unusual would feel bound to report it, just as I did. Besides, by now those Guides will be having a whale of a time telling all and sundry how they helped the police at the place where the murder was committed, and hunting for a knife must have given them a thrill which it would be ridiculous to expect them to keep to themselves.'

'Knives may not have been specified definitely, but I agree with your conclusions.'

'The murderer may have been among that knot of gawpers who were at the roadside watching operations when we arrived. I say, do you think there was something a bit fishy about my meeting Morpeth this morning?'

'In what way? She had two of the hounds with her and we know that the dogs were exercised daily by the sisters and Susan.'

'Exercising the hounds on that cliff path instead of on the open moor sounds a very unusual proceeding, especially as the path is narrow and so many holidaymakers use it.'

'I expect the hounds had already taken exercise on the open moor and that Morpeth had decided to walk into the near part of the valley and go home by the pleasantest route.'

'Well, do I ring up and ask about the hiker?'

'I think not. Let's talk first to the Rant Sisters. After that –'

'Jam tomorrow and jam yesterday, but never jam today,' said Laura. 'I was looking forward to getting a bit of exclusive information, but you know best.'

12

Information From Crozier Lodge

'I had better telephone Bryony and say that you want to see the sisters,' said Laura. 'How shall I put it?'

'Put it that we would like them to dine with us here tonight.'

'What about Susan? She usually has supper with them. Is she invited, too?'

'Certainly. Tell them half-past six for a seven o'clock dinner. If they accept, reserve a table for four or five. I have doubts whether Susan will accept.'

'Clothes, I suppose,' said Laura. 'People are so sensitive about appearing in public looking different from everybody else, but surely she's got a summer frock or something.'

Susan turned down the invitation. She did not like hotel food, Bryony reported. Laura offered to pick up the sisters and convey them to the hotel, but Bryony pointed out that they had their own car and that if Laura picked them up she would also feel compelled to drive them home later.

'Sorry about Susan,' said Laura, politely but insincerely, when she met them in the hotel vestibule. She had not taken much of a liking to the blunt-featured kennel-maid.

Dame Beatrice was more truthful than Laura had been. 'You will be able to talk more freely in Susan's absence,' she said. Bryony looked enquiringly at her and then asked whether the invitation had strings to it, a question which appeared to shock her sister, but which Dame Beatrice answered with equanimity. 'Certainly,' she said, 'but I hope you will enjoy your dinner none the less. The cooking here is excellent and the service good.'

'Since you are going to pump us, you are right in thinking that Susan's presence might have been embarrassing,' said Morpeth. 'She is not going back to her cottage tonight. She seems unusually nervous since she knew about the murder in the valley. She will barricade herself in our house with two of the hounds to keep her company and hope that we shall not be home too late.'

'Then,' said Laura impulsively and, this time, sincerely, 'I do wish she had come with you. It must be rotten to feel scared.'

'Yes,' agreed the tender-hearted Morpeth, 'we ought not to leave her too long alone in the house. Don't forget about the prowler and –'

'But we haven't seen or heard him lately,' said Bryony, 'and Susan will be quite all right with Osiris and Amon in the house.'

'What has to be said can be begun at the dinner-table and finished over coffee in the lounge,' said Dame Beatrice. 'It should not take long.'

'I am all apprehension,' said Morpeth.

'Don't be silly,' said her stronger-minded sister. 'What could Dame Beatrice have to talk about that should make you apprehensive?'

By nine o'clock the session was over, the questions had been asked and answered and the sisters were on their way home. So adroitly and tactfully had Dame Beatrice steered the conversation that not even Bryony realised how much had been revealed of life at Crozier Lodge before Dr Rant's death, Dr Mortlake's departure and the arrival of Susan.

That it had not been a happy household Dame Beatrice already knew, but there were details which, so far, had remained undisclosed. One of these was that, soon after he had taken the post of assistant to Dr Rant – it was never called a partnership – Mortlake had proposed marriage to Bryony.

Whether Bryony had ever thought of marriage up to that point she did not disclose, but apparently she had turned down the young doctor's offer with some firmness.

Dr Mortlake had received the dismissal of his proposal gracefully, but with a veiled indication that he had not given up hope and that the offer would be renewed later. This, however, stated Bryony, had not come about, for shortly afterwards Mrs Rant became very ill, so that during what everybody foresaw would be a terminal disorder, anything in the nature of lovemaking seemed to Bryony to be completely out of place and she had indicated this to Mortlake in ways which could not be misinterpreted.

After the death of his wife, Dr Rant had begun the course of alcoholism and drugs which led to his own death. More and more work depended upon Mortlake, especially after the death of Mrs Subbock, when the villagers refused to be attended by Rant – although the holidaymakers made no distinction between the two doctors except for those who came year after year and got to hear the rumours that Dr Rant was 'past it'.

'Of course, the end was inevitable, I suppose,' said Bryony, 'when he began prescribing drugs for himself and did not give up but, if possible, increased his consumption of alcohol.' He had become more and more tyrannical and unreasonable, and suffered from periods of morbid introspection.

'Do you happen to know when your father made his will?' asked Dame Beatrice.

'Oh, yes. He made a fresh will as soon as our mother's funeral was over. Everything had been left to her, you see. He was beastly to her, as he was to us, but he knew what was the right thing to do. Unluckily she died before he did, otherwise the three of us could have settled down to quite a happy, peaceful life, because there was no shortage of money, thanks to the rich old lady in Stafford.'

Bryony referred to the time when the Rant family had lived in the Midlands. The old lady, it seemed, had suffered from chronic bronchitis and often spoke of moving further south. Dr Rant was in constant attendance on her and persuaded her that to move from the comfortable, warm home she had always known and try to settle down among people she did not know and to have another doctor prescribe and care for her would not be to her advantage.

She died rather suddenly, and it was then discovered that she had left all her money to Rant. There were mutterings of undue influence among the members of charitable institutions which had hoped to benefit, but there were no relatives to contest the provisions of the will, neither could the charities prove that they had been promised anything.

However, ugly rumours began to circulate and, although nobody dared say so openly, it began to seep about that the old lady had shuffled off this mortal coil remarkably soon after the will had been signed and witnessed. The witnesses, two of the old lady's servants, were responsible for this undercover but dangerous hint and Dr Rant, at that time an able physician although even then a selfish husband and an unsympathetic father, had been forced to leave a rapidly declining practice and bury himself morosely in Abbots Crozier.

'I was fifteen when we moved south,' said Bryony, 'and Morpeth was twelve. We were overjoyed at first to live in the country and so near the sea. We went to boarding school and loved it. Some of the girls were not so keen and found the rules, especially those relating to being out-of-bounds, irksome and frustrating, but for us it was heaven after living with father and being toads under the harrow. I was heartbroken when he took me away to be a drudge at home. I was eighteen then. Morpeth stayed on for a couple of years, then she was also taken away from school and we had to resign ourselves to the fact that there was no chance for either of us to go to college or train for anything except to be father's slaves and watch mother's health getting worse and worse.'

It came out that Bryony, as the driver of the car, was sent regularly to the chemist's on behalf of her father. His prescriptions were made up by an elderly pharmacist in Castercombe who had died shortly after the demise of Dr Rant himself.

'I used to go by way of the road through the valley,' said Bryony, 'until it was blocked for weeks by a big fall of rock. After that, I had to drive down to Abbots Bay and take the coast road and come back the same way. I much preferred it, but, of course, it took a great deal longer and father used to be very impatient with me. In the end, Dr Mortlake heard him reproaching me in his usual hurtful manner – and, after that, Dr Mortlake took the prescriptions and told me to go out and enjoy myself. He would hand me the medicine (that's what father always called it) when he returned. He drives much faster and more confidently than I do, so he was able to cut down on the time and this mollified father, so we all bene-fited.'

'Didn't you ever think of leaving home?' asked Laura.

'With what? We had no money of our own while father was alive and we weren't trained for anything. Besides, there was mother. Even after her death, we were still helpless. If Dr Mortlake had been in a position to buy his own practice, I would have been tempted to accept his offer of marriage, but he was not in such a position. Besides, I knew he would never agree to have Morpeth to live with us, and I certainly would not have been willing to leave her on her own to cope with father.'

'I never liked Dr Mortlake,' said Morpeth, 'after I knew he wanted to take Bryony away from me. All the same, I some-times wonder whether we ought not to be very grateful to him.'

'In what way?' Laura enquired.

'Oh, after mother's death he did far more work for the practice than father did. Also, when he was with us – at meals, and so on, you know – father kept his temper in check where we were concerned and that was a very good thing.'

'A very interesting and informative evening, I thought,' said Dame Beatrice, when the sisters had returned to Crozier Lodge. 'What impression did it make on you?'

'I think Morpeth's gratitude to Dr Mortlake may rest upon something more than that his presence at meal-times kept Dr Rant in check to some extent. What a life those two women seem to have had of it, don't they? I'm certain, if I had been Bryony, I would have left home, money or no money, job or no job, especially after the mother died.'

Dame Beatrice nodded, but not in agreement. 'Bryony might have taken the risk of breaking away and trying a taste of freedom, but not with Morpeth acting as her Old Man of the Sea. It is clear that they have no intention of ever separating,' she said. 'There are several more questions I must ask the sisters, but they can wait until tomorrow.'

Dame Beatrice rang Crozier Lodge at half-past three the following afternoon, guessing that although Susan and one of the Rants might be out exercising hounds, it was unlikely that the Lodge would be untenanted. Morpeth answered the call.

'Do come to tea,' she said. 'The others will be back by half-past four and I've baked some lovely scones and there will be home-made strawberry jam and clotted cream.'

After tea, Dame Beatrice and Laura were introduced to the hounds. The bitches, including Sekhmet, who was never in *purdah*, were loose in the garden and responded politely and, in Sekhmet's case, enthusiastically to the visitors, but these were able to view the dogs only through the meshes of the strong wire fence which surrounded the stable yard. Dame Beatrice did not put her questions until she and Laura were about to take their leave. The two sisters accompanied them to the double gates outside which they had left the car, but Susan remained in the house, as Dame Beatrice had supposed that she would do, as the visitors were not, strictly speaking, her guests.

'I suppose,' said Dame Beatrice, 'that if either of you needed medical attention, you would call in Dr Mortlake.'

'Oh, no,' said Morpeth. 'He almost counts as a brother, you see. We should have the man from Axehead, but it hasn't been necessary since father died.'

'I can see that your father would have been unlikely to avail himself of his partner's services, particularly as Dr Mortlake can hardly have approved of certain aspects –'

'You mean the booze,' said Bryony, with a short laugh. 'Even less did he approve of the drugs or that father made up his own prescriptions for them.'

'He knew what the prescriptions were, of course?'

'I don't know, but he was kind enough to relieve me of the job of presenting them at the chemist's in Castercombe, so I think he was sure to have known something about what father had ordered,' Bryony said. 'I used to have to wait, quite often, before the bottle was ready to be handed over. It was a nuisance I was very glad to get rid of.'

'Did you see the chemist make up the prescriptions?' asked Dame Beatrice.'

'No, he used to do that in his back room, with the help of his chemist's boy, whom I never met. Apparently, he was an intelligent lad and took a great interest, Dr Mortlake told us, in the prescriptions, so the chemist, who was getting old, taught him quite a lot, although, of course, he had no proper training or qualifications. It's my belief, all the same, that he was trusted, in the end, to make up some of the medicines. Of course, nobody was supposed to know that, but rumours do get around.'

'But they weren't true,' said Morpeth. 'The old chemist would never have dared. You can't have an unqualified person making up prescriptions. You might kill somebody.'

'I was only repeating what I had heard. Anyway, the old chemist has gone and Dr Mortlake said the young man had gone, too. Perhaps he went abroad and practised his skills there. It's a pity to let talents go to waste.'

13

Brother and Sister

'So now for Susan,' said Dame Beatrice, when they were in the car. 'Drive down to the Axehead road, as usual, and then turn left and pull up where the zigzag footpath from Abbots Crozier ends in the middle of Abbots Bay village. There, I fear, we may have some time to wait.'

'We are to waylay her?'

'I do not want to visit her in her cottage, but I must see her alone. Before we can get any further in this business, she will have to explain why she left home so early on the day of the first man's death and what she was doing up to the time that Sekhmet was missing. The police are not satisfied, I am sure, with her continued assertion that she was bathing in the Abbots Bay sea-pool.'

'If she wasn't, and refuses to come clean, she's asking for trouble, but why are you bothering? We didn't know the first man and we certainly didn't take to that charlatan Ozymandias. You don't think Susan is likely to be pinched for the first death, do you?'

'She could also be apprehended for the second one now that those scalpels have been found, and so could Bryony or Morpeth.'

'I thought it was pretty clear the scalpels had been taken by that tramp, or whatever he was, who slept in the garage loft.'

'Or by the poacher, perhaps. As for the man in the loft, he may or may not have stolen the doctor's bag, but the poacher has identified him as the man Susan found dead at Watersmeet, so he could not have been the murderer of Goodfellow.'

'The poacher only recognised him on the strength of what could have been a very poor and misleading artist's impression.'

'That reminds me. Now that the local police and I are mutually acquainted, I must ask to see the far from poor and misleading pictures their official photographer took of the dead man which were thought to be too gruesome to print in the newspapers.'

'You don't think you know who he was, do you?'

'No. I am hoping that I can find someone to tell me.'

They sat on for half an hour and expected to wait longer, but Susan, it seemed, had left Crozier Lodge earlier than usual. Laura got out of the driver's seat and greeted her.

'Hullo, there!' she said. 'We've been waiting until we could get you on your own, away from Bryony and Morpeth. Hop into the car and have a word with Dame Beatrice.'

Dame Beatrice had taken her seat at the back. A bewildered but unexpectedly obedient Susan got in beside her. Her obedience was soon explained.

'I think I'm in for a spot of bother,' she said. 'The police don't believe that first death was an accident, do they?'

'The more one knows of Sekhmet, the less one can conceive of a man's being so much alarmed by her attentions as to yield up his trousers to her and dash into a river to escape from her. Have the police made her acquaintance?'

'Yes. They've been once or twice, a different man each time, and I was asked to go into the house so that her reactions wouldn't be conditioned by my presence.'

'In other words, to find out how she would behave herself with strangers when you were not there,' said Laura. 'What did the Rants think about these visits?'

'They don't know anything about them. That's what worries me. They must have kept watch and seen Bryony and Morpeth go out with four of the hounds, so that they knew I was alone at the Lodge with nobody to back me up. Of course, all that damn bitch did was to abase herself before them, pile on the charm, roll over, wag her stinking tail and more or less jump through hoops for their benefit. If ever a dog landed its handler and feeder in jug, that dog is blasted Sekhmet and that handler and feeder is me. Besides, now this second death – this obvious murder – has come about, the police are more on their toes than ever.'

'But you couldn't have any connection with the murder in the valley,' said Laura. 'It took place in the late evening. You would have been back in your cottage, not roaming the moor seeking whom you might devour.'

'That's all *you* know,' said Susan. 'I don't always go straight home from the Lodge. I'm not liked in the village but I do go quite often to the Crozier Arms. I've got my bit of money, and I like my pint and I don't see why unfriendliness should do me out of it.'

'I wonder you don't patronise a pub down here in Abbots Bay,' said Laura.

'Chance would be a fine thing. The chairman of the licensing justices owns both the big hotels here, and he sees to it that there's no pub, as such, in the place. Well, I'm not the type to feel at home in a hotel bar. I stink of dog, I suppose, and my clothes aren't exactly *haute couture*. At the Crozier Arms, they're not particular what you look or smell like, so long as you can pay your shot. I might be more popular there if I could stand my round, but, for one thing, I can't afford it and, for another, one pint is my limit. Sorry! I'm talking too much.'

'Far from that,' said Dame Beatrice. 'In fact, I hope that you will be prepared to tell us a great deal more.'

'Such as what?' Susan's mood, which had been expansive although slightly melancholy, changed. She became wary and suspicious.

Dame Beatrice sensed the change. She said gently, 'You need help. You have admitted that, but I cannot and I will not work in the dark. Where were you on the evening of Good-fellow's death?'

'I told you. I was in the Crozier Arms.'

'And after that?'

'Oh, well, I visited a friend.'

'The same friend as you visited on the morning of the Watersmeet death?'

Susan's expression turned to one of mulish obstinacy.

'How much do you know? – not that you'll tell me,' she said.

'Certainly I will tell you. All that I know is that you did not go for a bathe that morning. The rest is surmise.'

'Oh, yes? Well, that isn't much help to you because you wouldn't be right and I'm still not saying anything.'

'Not even if I mention a poacher named Adams?'

'The Rants pay for the rabbits and he's never been convicted for poaching or stealing or anything else.'

'And, so far, he has not been identified as your brother.'

'How did you find that out?' Susan blurted out the words in alarmed surprise.

'I mentioned that it was surmise, but my guesses are always based upon deduction, which is another way of saying that I am trained and experienced in putting two and two together. You may trust me. I know you have killed nobody.'

'Why?'

'Call it instinct.'

'You don't mean that,' said Susan, rousing herself as though she had been heartened, as indeed she had. 'I know your reputation for catching criminals. You know who the Crozier murderer is, don't you?'

'Do you?' asked Laura, when Susan, having told them a story which was an appendix to what they already knew, had got out of the car and gone home.

'Do I what?'

'Know who the murderer is.'

'So would you if you thought over all that we have been told, but, as usual, it is a question of proof, as Nicholas Blake has put it. However, I hope to learn from a little experiment I am going to make with the assistance of those Watersmeet photographs which were not published in the newspapers. Meanwhile, think of what we have been told.'

'Does Susan's story, the one she has just told us, come into it?'

'I think not, except that Dr Rant died and that some time after his death, when the Rant sisters decided to breed Pharaohs, Susan became kennel-maid to Sekhmet and the cherished hounds.'

'You said she was not the murderer, but you mention Dr Rant. You don't mean that *Dr Rant* was also murdered, do you?'

'If he was not, my whole theory falls to the ground.'

Laura did not voice the astonishment she felt, but, as she drove homewards, she turned the conversation on to the story they had heard from Susan. They had known that she had been adopted by the vicar of Axehead and the twin villages of Abbots Crozier and Abbots Bay, and that her tiny income came from interest on the money he had left her in his will. They also knew that she remembered a brother. In the account she had just given them, she said that she had lost track of him after she became a member of the vicar's household, for, as a child, she was not allowed to write to him and when she was old enough to decide such matters for herself, she found that the home where they had been fostered together had been vacated and she could find nobody who could tell her where the inmates had gone. She did not pursue her enquiries very far, for she reasoned that her brother would be old enough to be at work and could be anywhere in the British Isles or even in Canada or Australia or some other part of the globe. In any case, they had never, as children, been very close friends, so, having made some attempt to trace him and failed, she soon gave up the quest and, after the deaths of her adoptive parents, whose surname she had taken, she occupied herself by taking seasonal jobs in the hotels of Abbots Bay and Abbots Crozier and in such occupations as baby-sitting to families in Axehead, where there was a repertory theatre and a dance hall, or as an auxiliary worker in the Axehead hospital. She had also worked in the kennels of the moorland hunt and, later, for a veterinary surgeon in Castercombe, so when she discovered that the Rant sisters were keeping and occasionally breeding Pharaoh hounds, she had found, in her own words, 'my life's work and a couple of good friends, if only they would have me'.

Her complete independence, however, she did not abandon, for she felt, wisely, no doubt, that some of Dr Rant's imperiousness had been bred into Bryony and that to maintain a certain amount of *apartheid* from the sisters was the policy to be followed. The arrangement suited all three. The sisters were happy to have Crozier Lodge to themselves each evening and Susan's help was invaluable when they first took on the Pharaoh hounds. Susan retained her own little home and steadfastly refused any money payment for her services, though the sisters insisted on feeding her.

All this came out in Susan's story and so did the explanation of her suspect activities on the morning of the Watersmeet death and her subsequent refusal to disclose to the police where she had been before she showed up at Crozier Lodge and found that Sekhmet was missing.

'What made you go to Sekhmet's kennel before you went up to the house?' Dame Beatrice had asked. 'Such was not your custom, was it?'

'I have a keener sense of smell than either of the Rants,' Susan had replied, 'and I detected the smell of aniseed the moment I got inside the gates. I went straight to the stable yard, but the hounds were all right, although, of course, very restless and excited because they could smell the aniseed, too, so then I thought I had better check on Sekhmet. I couldn't imagine anybody wanting to steal her, but Morpeth valued her and it was no secret that the Rants had money, so Morpeth might have offered quite a sizeable reward to get the dog back. That was the way I reasoned.'

'That won't quite do,' said Dame Beatrice. 'You have nothing to lose by being frank with me. Let us forget the aniseed and come to what you were doing before you reached Crozier Lodge.'

The rest of Susan's story had followed. It was some weeks after she had joined Bryony and Morpeth that she encountered the poacher Adams, and it was not until Bryony mentioned his name and remarked how useful it was when he brought along rabbits for the hounds that she realised the poacher's name was the same as that which she had been made to abandon when the vicar and his wife adopted her.

'They wanted me to feel that I was their very own daughter,' Susan said, 'and that I would be proud to take their name. I don't know about being proud,' she added, addressing Laura rather than Dame Beatrice, 'but it gave me a feeling of safety which was heaven after feeling so lost. They treated us quite well at the Home, but it was impersonal, if you know what I mean. You didn't feel as though you belonged anywhere and my brother and I were separated, I thought for ever, once I was adopted and went to live at the vicarage, and we never met after that until the day I first opened the back door to him at Abbots Crozier. He didn't know who I was then, and he doesn't now. I have never told him I am his sister. Snobbishness, I suppose, but not everybody wants to claim relationship with the village poacher. But every now and then, when my bit of interest comes in, I buy him a shirt or a jacket or trousers from a jumble sale. That's where I was that morning, taking him a lovely wool shirt that I had picked up the previous week. He may be a poacher and perhaps a bit of a thief, but he's a decent man and I like to think I've got somebody belonging to me, even if they themselves don't know it.'

'Well, I am deeply affected by this artless tale,' said Dame Beatrice briskly and without irony, 'but it does not explain, so far as I am concerned, a point of some importance. What did you do when you found that Adams was not at home when you called?'

'I guessed he was out rabbiting. I had plenty of time before I needed to show up at Crozier Lodge and I wanted to give him my present personally, so I hung about on the moor until he came back. It wasn't all that long to wait. I gave him the shirt but asked him to say nothing about it to anybody – '

'Did he never wonder why you offered him these kind-nesses?'

'He thought they were because I had been brought up in a vicarage and was accustomed to doing acts of charity. We never wrote to one another after we were separated, as I told you, so, although I suppose he had heard I was not the vicar's own child, he had no idea that I was his sister because of the change of name.'

'So, when you met him that morning, he told you that he had left the rabbits in the postbox and that somebody had walked off with Sekhmet,' said Laura. 'Simple, when you know the answer. So that's why you went straight to Sekhmet's kennel before you went up to the house.'

'That's about the size of it.'

'Why on earth didn't you tell the police what you had done and where you had been, instead of letting them suspect you and search your cottage?'

'She has answered that,' said Dame Beatrice. 'She did not want a connection made between her and Adams.'

'I should have told them if things had got worse for me,' said Susan. 'I was pretty badly scared when they did search the cottage and found that ridiculous hat. I knew then what I had suspected all along.'

'That the man in the river had been murdered?'

'Oh, I had had my suspicions before that. Nobody could have got that deep gash in his head from slipping and hitting his head on one of those rounded boulders. It wasn't so much the police I was scared of. It was the murderer. Nobody else could have palmed off that silly hat on me. He must have spied on me at Watersmeet, I think, and that's a horrible thought.'

'How much of her story is true, do you suppose?' asked Laura later. Dame Beatrice shook her head.

'We can check a good deal of it with Adams without giving away his relationship to Susan, since she is sensitive about that.'

'Don't you think he has put two and two together by now?'

'That is more than likely. Several points in her story are inconsistent. Susan is not very good at deceit. What I *do* think is that a shop in Axehead has found a fine woollen shirt missing from its stock. Such items are expensive and I think would be beyond the reach of Susan's purse.'

'You don't mean she nicked it!'

'She felt that the end justified the means, no doubt. I have heard that the Jesuits hold similar views, although they do not express them by stealing woollen shirts from haberdashers.'

'Anyway, if the rest of the story is true, we know where she went that morning and why she went to Sekhmet's kennel before going to the house, so those are two niggling little points cleared up, not that they matter, but I do hate unsolved mysteries and one can't do with them in a case of murder,' said Laura. 'Shall you go and see Adams?'

'Not at present and perhaps not at all. And now, to play havoc with the ballad of Sir Patrick Spens, where shall I find a skeely sculptor to model this head of mine?'

'Yours?'

'No. The head of the man found in the river. The police photographed it full-face and in profile. It will be hard if we cannot find somebody to model him, taking, we'll say, three years off his age and restoring his appearance to what it was before he was attacked so brutally.'

'So you *do* know who the Watersmeet man was?'

'Dear me, no, but from a bow drawn at a venture the arrow sometimes finds a rare and valuable quarry.'

14

Full Marks For Artistic Impression

'Signor Tussordiano,' said Laura, looking up from her cross-word puzzle that evening after they had spoken with Susan.

'I beg your pardon?' said Dame Beatrice.

'That waxworks man who used to travel the fairs with all those heads of murderers. The police arrested him because they thought he had killed his wife, but you proved it was a drunken lion-tamer with whom she was having an affair.'

'Dear me, yes, but how do you know? You were not with me then.'

'No, I was teaching a class of forty wary-skulled young ladies who were only killing time until they were old enough to leave school, poor perishers. I wonder why headmistresses always give the rottenest class to the newest recruit? Anyway, old Tusso would model that head for you and be glad to do it. I'll put matters in train to track him down, shall I? Gavin will know who keeps the tabs on these people. What's the good of having a husband at Scotland Yard if one can't make use of him? Anyway, to answer your question, after you left Cartaret College, which was alleged to train teachers and failed sig-nally, so far as I was concerned, to carry out its function, I followed your career with avid interest. If it isn't a rude answer, why did you pick me for your dogsbody when the other one left to get married?'

Dame Beatrice considered the question and then said that she did not know. She returned to the point at issue. 'Signor Tussordiano?' she said. 'But what an excellent idea!'

'We like to earn our salary. OK, then, I'll get busy. One

thing about Tusso, he won't ask any questions you don't want to answer.'

The exhibitor of waxwork heads was a white-haired old gentleman with the innocent eyes which Dame Beatrice associated with jewel thieves and the sellers of shares in bogus oil wells and copper mines. However, Signor Tussordiano was almost as innocent as he looked. His real name was Pugh and he was apt to talk nostalgically of what he referred to as 'the valley', although actually he had been born in Deptford and had never been further west than St Giles's Fair in Oxford, and that was in his early boyhood when his uncle had first taken him on the road.

Laura had been right, on the whole, when she had stated that he would ask no awkward questions. He did put one query to Dame Beatrice when she told him what she hoped he could do for her.

'Murderer?' he asked eagerly, when she showed him the photographs. 'One for my collection?'

'Murdered, we think, not a murderer,' she replied. 'I hope, with your expert help, to get him identified, and that, perhaps, will lead us to the killer.'

'Nice big pictures,' he said, spreading out the newspaper. 'You can make out the underlying bone structure and that's what matters. These photos would be about a quarter natural size, I reckon. Call back in a week and I'll have summat for you. I'll have to charge you for the materials, but, seeing what you done for me in the past, I'll do the work free. I s'pose I couldn't 'ave the 'ead when you've done with it? Then when you've cotched the murderer I can model his head as well and set 'em up side by side.'

'Certainly you may have it.' So the bargain was struck. Dame Beatrice advanced the money the old man said he would need and she and Laura returned to the Stone House. It had been agreed that the modeller would telephone when the head was ready. Dame Beatrice had been to Crozier Lodge to obtain details of the dead man's colouring with regard to hair and eyes, and she had checked with the police to make certain that Susan's memory was not at fault. Inspector Burfield, who had been the officer responsible for having the body removed from the river, had confirmed Susan's description, but added that, as the man's head had been more or less submerged when he was found, his hair was probably not so dark as Susan had described it. 'More mid-brown than nearly black' was the inspector's emendation of her description.

'So you've given the old chap an idea,' said Laura. 'I like the thought of setting a murderer's head side by side with that of his victim. His collection doesn't go further back than Crippen and his dissected wife with the operation scar, but he can do Emily Kaye to pair up with Patrick Mahon and one of those unfortunate females to team with Neill Cream.'

'You show a regrettable and ghoulish relish for your theme. I shall be interested to see what Signor Tussordiano produces for us.'

When she was shown the modelled head, Dame Beatrice was doubtful whether her plan would work. She was presented with the bust of a young man which appeared to have no connection whatever with the photographs she had supplied to Tussordiano. The dead man's eyes had been staring and wide open. Those of the model were open in the normal way and one had a slight cast in it. The mouth in the photograph was also open, as though the man had been in the act of saying something – to the bitch Sekhmet, most likely – when he was struck down. The side of his face that had been shattered had been completely reconstructed in the model; the lips were slightly parted and the modeller had given the immature face a leering expression which, together with the cast in the left eye, gave the viewer anything but a pleasing impression of the subject's character.

'In fact,' said Laura, 'if you were told that this was the murderer instead of the murderee, you could well believe it.'

'Yes, hardly a prepossessing countenance,' agreed Dame Beatrice. However disappointing the first result of her experiment seemed to be, she decided to carry out her plan. She had the painted waxwork photographed in colour and from various angles before she returned it, as promised, to Tussordiano and then began her quest for information about the somewhat repulsive-looking youth which the photographs portrayed. Laura had supposed that George, the reliable chauffeur and general handyman, would be handed copies of the pictures to take to the Crozier Arms and the public houses in Axehead, and she was surprised when Dame Beatrice did not avail herself of George's services, but told Laura to drive her to Castercombe.

It was a handsome town founded by the Romans on four crossroads much after the pattern of Cirencester. It went one better than the Cotswold town in that it had acquired under the Normans a cathedral in place of Cirencester's memorable parish church of St John the Baptist with its gloriously over-ornate south porch and magnificent fifteenth-century tower; and Castercombe had a covered market in place of the open square in the town centre at Cirencester.

Laura asked no questions. She possessed the Highlander's courteous but almost instinctive dislike of enquiring into other people's business or motives. When her college friend, Kitty Trevelyan, had enquired the reason for this reticence, Laura had replied that what you did not know, you did not have to do anything about. This reply, Laura remembered with a non-Presbyterian grin, had shocked the High Anglican Kitty, who had demanded, 'But, Dog, don't you have any sort of a conscience?'

'Can't afford one,' Laura had responded. 'Your lot may be the Conservative Party at prayer, but our lot were brought up to quote Dr Johnson.'

'As how? All he said was that the lady smelt and he stank. I shouldn't have thought that was the sort of remark you made in Early Victorian drawing-rooms.'

'In eighteenth-century drawing-rooms, ducky.'

'Well, what about what he said about your lot?'

'You ought to be made to analyse and parse that observation. Anyway, he asked where else would you find such horses and such men. He was talking about oats.'

'Wild ones?'

'No, fathead, the kind you eat.'

'Well, even those you have to sow, I suppose,' Kitty had said, 'so it comes to the same thing in the end.'

'Dear old Kitty,' thought Laura nostalgically, as she took the one-in-four gradient down the Axehead hill into Abbots Bay and then followed the coast road to Castercombe. 'Made a fortune in the hairdressing and the fashion businesses, and married a rich man into the bargain. He adored her and her idiocy and maintains that she was his inspiration. Who says fools don't prosper?'

Having parked the car in one of the marked spaces in what had been the old marketplace in Castercombe, she waited for further instructions.

'Half-past one,' said Dame Beatrice. 'Lunch, I think. You must be famished, as we breakfasted so early. Did I not perceive a likely-looking hostelry as we turned into this square? Would you care to walk over to it and find out whether they can put a table at our disposal?'

Lunch over, she produced her photographs and displayed them to the receptionist. The girl said she had only lived in the town for a year, so Dame Beatrice asked if there was anyone on the staff of the hotel who had been living or working there at least three years previously. She added that the subject of the pictures was unlikely to have been a guest staying at the hotel, but that somebody on the staff might have known him if that person had been resident in the town.

'Try Fred in the cocktail lounge,' said the girl. 'He's been here longest.' She looked appraisingly at Dame Beatrice's eccentric but obviously expensive clothes and at Laura's well-cut summer suit and asked, 'Come into a fortune, has he, this young fellow?'

Dame Beatrice cackled, thanked the girl and made for the

cocktail lounge with her photographs. Here she ordered two brandies and asked the elderly barman what he would have. His was a small port in which he pledged the ladies' health. Dame Beatrice asked him if he had ever known the young man in the pictures which she handed to him. He looked at them carefully, but shook his head.

'Not without he worked for Parrish's the chemist,' he said. 'I might have seen him in there, if I recollect. I'll tell you who would likely know for sure, and that's my brother Bert, as keeps a do-it-yourself shop in Paternoster Way, along by the cathedral. Always in and out of the chemist's in his younger days owing to suffering with his stomach. Then he got Christian Science and give up the physic. About four or five year ago, you say. Ah, well, now, if anybody would recognise them pictures, Bert would. Ask for Mr Smallwood if his assistant's minding the counter. They close for dinner-time, but he'll be open again by now and most likely having his after-dinner snooze while the assistant runs the shop. There ain't much doing in his line in the early afternoons. His trade is mostly on Saturdays and in the evenings when chaps come by on their way home from work.'

The cathedral was so much of a landmark that Dame Beatrice and Laura found Paternoster Way without difficulty. Laura opened the door of the do-it-yourself shop and saw that it was in the charge of a young man wearing a brown overall. She came out and reported that brother Bert was not visible, so was probably sleeping off his lunch.

'Then we will not disturb him for a while,' said Dame Beatrice. 'I want him to be in sunny mood when I show him the photographs. We will visit the cathedral. I admire large, gloomy buildings erected to the glory of God and as a passport to heaven for those who built, paid for and maintain them.'

The interior was certainly grand enough and gloomy enough to satisfy her. She spent most of the time seated in one of the pews near the end of the nave and studied the architecture, the transition from Norman to Early English, the fourteenth-century east window, the fan vaulting of the chancel and the carved stone screen which separated the nave from the choir.

Laura wandered around identified piscinas and aumbrys, the ornate fifteenth-century tomb surmounted by the effigy of the bishop who had been responsible for the later alterations to the building, found a little locked door which had led to the rood stair and examined the stone screen in greater detail than Dame Beatrice was able to do from her seat in the nave.

She came back to her employer and announced that she wanted a postcard or two from the stand by the south door. After this, they went into the cloister and the chapter house and then Dame Beatrice looked at her watch and decided that it was time they returned to Bert Smallwood's shop. Laura opened the door of it again; this time two men, one of them elderly, were there.

Laura, already briefed, spent some time in selecting an assortment of screws and a plastic arm for opening and closing a casement window, bought some emery paper and a pair of nail scissors, while Dame Beatrice wandered around inspecting the stock and then bought some metal clips for which she had no use whatever and a set of curtain hooks.

Having thus prepared the ground for negotiations of a different kind, she produced the photographs. The result was gratifying, particularly when she mentioned that Bert's brother Fred had sent her. The elderly man hardly did more than glance at the pictures.

'Why, that looks like young Todhunter,' he said. 'Used to work at Parrish's the chemist till he got the sack for putting his hand in the till. Went abroad, so I heard. I used to go regular to Parrish's before I saw the light and my stomach stopped playing me up.' The old man looked at her with curiosity and asked, 'Is he back here, then? Had trouble with him, have you?'

'Personally, no. I have never even met him.' She took another picture from the briefcase she was carrying. 'Could you recognise this as the same man photographed recently by the Axehead police?'

He went white when he saw the disfigured face of the dead man, but gave the picture far more attention than he had given to the photographs of the head which Tussordiano had modelled and then he shook his own.

'Could be,' he said, 'but I wouldn't like to swear to it. This one is dead, then?'

'Yes,' said Dame Beatrice. She produced her Home Office credentials. 'The police are interested in him, so I hope that you will be prepared to co-operate if they ask you to substantiate your recognition of the youth you knew as Todhunter. There is more than a suspicion that his death was no accident. That is why the police are so anxious to get him identified.'

'I've never had dealings with the police and I don't want to begin at my age.'

'You could sell your story to the papers, Mr Smallwood,' said his assistant. 'They pay big money for stories about murder.'

Before they left Castercombe, Dame Beatrice and Laura, having asked to be directed to the chemist's at which Todhunter had been an assistant, obtained no confirmation of Smallwood's identification of the model in the coloured photographs, for the shop had changed hands. Nevertheless, as Laura said, there was now something to report to the Axehead police. The detective-inspector was interested but cautious. He did not see, he said, that the identification of young Todhunter got him very much further in identifying the body of the man found in the river, since nobody had yet come forward to put a firm name to this man. They could not be certain he and Todhunter were the same.

'If the young fellow went abroad,' he said, 'we should have the devil of a job proving that he ever came back, especially as we don't know to what part of the world he went. Then, again, if this shopkeeper in Castercombe recognised the youngster in your photograph, but can't swear to the man in ours, well, there you are. In any case, we haven't a clue as to why anybody should murder him, any more than we know why Goodfellow was murdered. What's your theory, ma'am?'

'I believe the man in the river knew of something in the murderer's past and that the man found dead in the valley had been a witness of the river murder.'

'Ingenious, ma'am, but where is the proof?'

'Still to be sought.'

'Do you know who the murderer is?'

'Not, as you point out, without proof. I was told that young Todhunter was dismissed from his job for petty pilfering. Did the shopkeeper give him in charge as well, I wonder? If so, the police at Castercombe might also be able to identify my photograph and (a remote possibility, no doubt) recognise the man in yours.'

'Well, I'll get in touch with them, of course, since you suggest it, but, in my opinion, it's a very long shot, ma'am.'

It turned out that there had been no charge laid against Todhunter, but the Castercombe police agreed to find out what they could and whether the youth had indeed left the town. If he had, they would do their best to discover where he had gone and whether he had got into any trouble or made any enemies there, but they indicated that it was a forlorn hope.

'And, if he changed his name as, being in disgrace, he most likely did,' they said, 'we shall be left without a clue and and it might seem a waste of time and trouble to start looking into things now that he's dead.' The detective-inspector transmitted this opinion to Dame Beatrice when he received it and added that, great though he knew her reputation to be, even she would find this particular nut too hard to crack. Meekly she agreed.

'Are you *really* giving up?' asked Laura. Dame Beatrice cackled, but made no other reply. Meanwhile the police continued with their enquiries into the antecedents of the so-far mysterious Goodfellow and with some, although limited, success. To Bryony's annoyance, Susan's curiosity and Morpeth's alarm, they began at Crozier Lodge just as lunch was being cleared away, so that all three women were in the house. Detective-Inspector Harrow began with Susan, but the interview produced nothing. She denied, quietly but firmly, ever having met Goodfellow.

'I've been told about him, of course,' she said, 'but the only time he came here I was out with a couple of the hounds and when I got back I was told about his visit and what a screwball he seemed to be. Scared both the girls, I guess, so Bryony wished him on to Dame Beatrice, she being trained to deal with such cases and, so far as my knowledge goes, he never came here again.'

15

Watersmeet Again

'There is something I ought to tell you,' said Bryony. Dame Beatrice looked interested and nodded.

'A confession of sorts,' she said. 'I have been expecting it, although I have no idea at all of what is about to be disclosed.'

'I did it with the best of intentions.'

'One so often does.'

'It's about that Watersmeet business. I know it was murder. I know what the murder weapon was and where it is.'

'Have you told the police?'

'No. They will be so angry with me that I am quite alarmed at the thought. I believe they could put me in prison for withholding evidence and concealing a murder weapon.'

'No doubt you had a reason for what you did. You spoke of good intentions.'

'Oh, yes, of course I had a reason. I thought Susan had done it. She found Sekhmet and the body. I thought perhaps she had seen the man kicking Sekhmet or something of that sort, and had attacked him with a sharp piece of flint. I found it – or, rather, one of the dogs did.' Bryony proceeded to tell the story of how curiosity had taken her to Watersmeet and of the hole in the bank which had interested the hound.

Dame Beatrice listened and did not interrupt. At the end of Bryony's confession she said, 'So why do you now think that Susan is innocent?'

'Oh, because whoever killed that man at Watersmeet must be the valley murderer. That stands to reason. Susan has an alibi for the whole evening on which Goodfellow was murdered. She was here for supper and we had it later than usual. She spent the rest of the evening at the Crozier Arms. She told us she did and I was mean enough to check. Regrettably, in a way, she got very drunk and the poacher Adams took her home and put her to bed. He seemed to think it was a good joke. I checked again, because it seemed very necessary in view of my previous suspicions, and it seems they made so much noise that they disturbed her neighbours, so there are witnesses.'

'Susan has now told me where she was at the time of the Watersmeet death, too, and I believe her. I am sure that Susan is not a murderess. I have almost enough evidence to convict the same person of both the crimes.'

'I suppose I mustn't ask – '

'Better not. I should not answer you at this juncture. We had better go and find the Watersmeet weapon, don't you think? If it was a sharp piece of flint, it should be identifiable among the other stones in the river.'

'The police will be so angry with me,' repeated Bryony unhappily.

'Then let me bear the brunt. Laura and I will go to Watersmeet and retrieve this talisman and bear our sheaves rejoicing to the Axehead police station.'

'You will have to involve me, of course.'

'Not unless you are a murderess,' said Dame Beatrice, with a grim cackle, 'but, if you were, you would hardly have come to me with this somewhat belated confession.'

'Remorse might have overtaken me.'

'Well, it has, but only because you now know that your suspicions of Susan were unjustified, although, to my mind, they were reasonable enough. I shall not involve you with the police if I can help it. After all, the piece of flint can hardly of itself identify the guilty party.'

'Would the running water have washed away fingerprints?'

'Yours and those of the murderer? As neither of you is likely to have had your fingerprints taken by the police, the question is immaterial at present.'

'Do you know who the murderer is, then?'
'I think I do, but actual proof is missing.'
'Will he or she murder anybody else?'
'Myself, perhaps, but that has been my occupational hazard for so many years that I have ceased to regard it as important.'

'If I may be permitted the question,' said Laura, 'why did you tell Bryony that we wanted to borrow Sekhmet and take her to Watersmeet with us? You don't suppose she will dash into the stream and retrieve this piece of flint, do you?'
'It is merely to check a statement. We have been told that the dog will go along with anybody who speaks kindly to her. I am relying on you to find out whether that is correct. Furthermore, I trust that you will go prepared to wade into the river and attempt to locate this piece of flint.'
'Don't you think the murderer may have gone there and located it and removed it?'
'No. According to Bryony's story, it had been hidden in a hole in the riverside bank. He or she – I refer to the guilty party – may have gone back with the intention of retrieving the piece of flint, but would have found it had disappeared from where it had been hidden. I doubt whether it would have occurred to him to look for it in the river. In any case, I doubt whether he will have gone back for it yet. He will let time pass and the story die down.'
'But by that time there won't be any point in finding it. It could no longer be dangerous to him.'
Dame Beatrice hummed the air of *Among My Souvenirs*. Laura looked hopefully at her, but received no satisfaction. She said, harking back to a previous subject, 'And supposing Sekhmet won't be cajoled into coming with me?'
'Then we were given unproven information, for the dog *did* know the person who led her away that morning.'
Laura tried again.
'Why didn't the murderer chuck the piece of flint into the river instead of hiding it in a hole? Did he think the police

might search the riverbed and find it?'

'I think not. I think he wanted to be sure that he himself could find it again when, as I said, all the local interest in the death had died down and he could safely retrieve it.'

'Well, no doubt it all makes sense, but not to me,' said Laura. 'If he wanted to keep the thing, why didn't he take it away with him?'

'He was afraid to do so, I imagine, in case, by some freak of fate, it should be traced to his possession. It is so true that conscience doth make cowards of us all.'

'He's going to get a nasty jolt when he dives into that hole and finds the flint gone.'

'He is going to get a nasty jolt, as you put it, long before that, I fancy,' said Dame Beatrice. 'Those who try to throw dust into other people's eyes are likely to blind themselves if the wind happens to be blowing the wrong way. Well, to find out whether we have been told the truth about Sekhmet's friendly way with strangers, I shall leave it to you to open negotiations with her. Make sure that no one from Crozier Lodge is with you when you make advances to the animal.'

Sekhmet fulfilled the predictions made about her. She received Laura with mindless enthusiasm, tore twice round what once had been the lawn at Crozier Lodge and then crouched adoringly at Laura's feet while a lead borrowed from Bryony was attached to her collar. Dame Beatrice had waited beside the car which Laura had parked outside the gate. She patted the now quiescent dog and the three of them walked towards the little bridge over the river.

Laura had picked up two things from the car before they left it. One article was a carrier bag containing a pair of rope-soled canvas shoes, the other was a small, light, canvas-seated garden chair. The shoes were to be worn when she waded in the river, the chair was for Dame Beatrice to occupy while Laura was searching for the piece of flint, a business which she guessed might take some time.

'Let Sekhmet loose,' said Dame Beatrice, when they had

crossed the bridge and were on the rough riverside path. 'She knows the spot we want and will lead us to it.'

'Bryony described it as being only a few yards below the confluence of the two streams,' said Laura. 'Wonder what Sekhmet was doing when the murderer hit the other fellow over the head?'

'She may well have been tethered to a tree and released when the deed had been done, the victim's trousers removed and the body dumped, alive or dead, in the river.'

'After the piece of flint had been hidden in the bank where Bryony found it?'

'Yes. She had then been released, given the pair of trousers and told to guard them, I think. We can test that when you give her your walking shoes to mind.'

'Thanks very much! And supposing she won't give them up when I want to change back into them? Still, anything in a good cause, I suppose.'

She released the dog, which disappeared immediately into the undergrowth. The two women walked on, Laura giving a whistle occasionally to which Sekhmet responded by making a brief, polite manifestation of herself before resuming her quest for rabbits.

'I wish our errand weren't quite so grim,' said Laura. 'It's lovely along here and the last setting on earth for a cowardly murder.'

'Yes, indeed,' Dame Beatrice agreed. 'There is a good deal to be said for the discovery of dead bodies in libraries rather, than in beauty spots.'

They had risen very early and had set out for Abbots Crozier in time, they hoped, to reach Watersmeet before the holiday makers found it. Fortunately it was more of an afternoon than a morning walk for most people and they encountered nobody of human kind. They were accompanied, however, by a robin, but whether in friendship or because he wanted to see them off his territory they did not know.

'I think it must be somewhere about here that Bryony

meant,' said Laura a little later. She unfolded the garden chair. 'If you'd like to sit here while I go paddling – ' she added. 'I should like to identify that hole in the bank Bryony mentioned. It must be quite close at hand. Ought we to have brought her with us after all?'

'I think not,' said Dame Beatrice, testing the small chair for firmness and then seating herself. 'Enjoy your search. I do not suppose the hole will tell us anything new, but time is of no object and this is a pleasant spot.'

Laura whistled up Sekhmet and this time the dog stayed with her. With the Labrador at her heels, she combed the bank. The hedge which crowned it was ragged and untended. Laura identified, in one part, the trailing wild rose with its white, wide-open flowers and, further along, there was the long-styled rose, stout-stemmed, erect and well foliaged, but of the dog rose, Laura's favourite, there was no sign, since the soil was not suited to it. However, on her walk along the cliff path she had seen the burnet rose in flower in its chosen habitat near the sea.

It was Sekhmet who found the hole. Laura was wearing a short-sleeved shirt. She put her hand and then her arm into the hole while the dog, suspecting the presence of rabbits, nuzzled against her trouser-leg quivering with anticipation.

'No droppings, so no rabbits, you idiot,' said Laura, 'in fact, no nothing.' She continued to search the bank, but there was no comparable hole, so, accompanied by the disillusioned dog, she returned to Dame Beatrice and the sunshine, which flecked with light the turbulent little river.

She took off her walking shoes, substituted for them the pair of rope-soled sand shoes, rolled her trouser legs up to above her knees and waded in at a nearby spot where the edge of the stream shelved gently into the water.

This was extremely cold, but the rope-soled shoes gave her a reasonable chance of keeping her footing on the wet stones and boulders of the riverbed. Now and again she would pick up a pebble, inspect it and let it fall. Dame Beatrice watched placidly and Sekhmet watched anxiously from the bank. The water splashed joyously over the rocks, and the robin, which had accompanied the seeker all the time that she was exploring the bank, actually perched for a moment on the wooden arm of Dame Beatrice's garden chair.

'I remind myself of the chap who got so bored and frustrated looking for the touchstone which turned everything to gold that he realised that he must have found it earlier on and chucked it away without looking at it,' said Laura, throwing down a pebble and coming out on to the bank.

'You are walking against the flow of the stream,' said Dame Beatrice. 'Why don't you try higher up and walk down this way?'

'Because I don't much want to take a ducking. The stream is running fast so near the confluence and the stones are slippery. The rush of water against the backs of my legs could upset my equilibrium. Still, if you say so.' She walked away from Dame Beatrice and up the slope before she stepped into the river again. This time, although her stance was precarious, her efforts met with success. She gave a shout and held up a piece of stone. Sekhmet, aware of drama, barked excitedly.

Two early strollers came along the path, the vanguard to several others. Dame Beatrice resurrected a small towel from the bag she had with her and vacated the chair so that Laura could sit down and dry her hands, arms, legs and feet. The newcomers gave the two women a cursory glance and passed on. Laura put on her walking shoes (in which, incidentally, Sekhmet had shown not the slightest interest) and then carefully dried the piece of flint.

'Here is a thing and a very pretty thing,' she said, handing it over to Dame Beatrice. 'Matters begin to add up. That is not a casual chunk of stone. It's been worked over.'

'It is a particularly fine example of what the *Cambridge Book of Ancient History* calls a *coup de poing*, but we wait to examine your find until after we have returned Sekhmet to her owners and Bryony has had a chance to confirm that we have the object she hid in the river.' They followed this plan and then picked up the car from the gates of Crozier Lodge and returned to the Stone House. Here they closely examined the piece of flint. It had been painstakingly and beautifully shaped, with feather-edged flaking and sharp, straight edges to the blade. It had obviously been intended by its neolithic fabricator as a dagger, for although at one end it had been fined down to a sharpish point, the other end had been smoothed and rounded and was intended to be grasped in the fist.

There was no trace of blood on the flint dagger. If ever there had been, Bryony or the murderer or the action of the running water had cleaned it off. Laura said, 'Of course we have no proof of where it came from and who owned it.'

'No, that is true. The first thing, I think, is to get the pathologist's opinion. We need to verify our own suspicions that this could have been the Watersmeet murder weapon.'

'Does that mean digging up the corpse?'

'The photographs may prove our point, but our course is to present the flint implement and leave the decisions to those who are qualified to make them. I shall suggest, however, that the Home Office pathologist is asked to give a second opinion to that of the county man and it may mean that he will insist upon an exhumation. After all, we are dealing with two cases of murder – three, in fact, if my deductions have not misled us – and the more evidence we can produce to lead the police to the guilty party the better.'

'I'm a bit surprised that you're so keen to hunt down this chap,' said Laura. 'You think he was being blackmailed by one of those he's killed and I know what you think of black-mailers.'

'It is on account of Bryony that I am concerned. She tried to hide the murder weapon, this flint artefact, and it was she who, after her father's death, most irresponsibly transferred the scalpels to the loft above the garage, where, as we have seen, any ill-disposed person could obtain access to them. She is an intelligent young woman and now that we have shown her the *coup de poing* for what it is, it will not take her long to put two and two together and come to the correct conclusion as to who owns it. Once she does that, I would not go bail for her safety. A person who has killed three is not likely to burke at a fourth, particularly if he has something against her already.'

'You say ''he''. Can it be that you are certain that the murderer is a man, not a woman?'

'When in doubt, the masculine pronoun covers both sexes,' said Dame Beatrice aggravatingly.

16

Exhumations

In different locations, but on the same subject, four conversations had been carried on.

'If that is what Dame Beatrice suggests,' said Sir Ranulph, the Home Office forensic expert, 'we had better have both the coffins up.'

'I hardly think much can be discovered in the case of Dr Rant which did not come out at the inquest,' said the county pathologist. 'The man drank and doped himself to death. The evidence at the inquest was quite clear and the coroner's direction to the jury was the only possible one. I had examined the body and both the police doctor and I concurred in our findings. I cannot think why Dame Beatrice entertains any suspicions. Given the facts, she cannot query them.'

'The fact remains that she *has* queried them. More than that, I understand the police were not altogether satisfied with the outcome.'

'That is true in the case of this man who died at Watersmeet, not in the case of Dr Rant.'

'Several people benefited from Dr Rant's death, though, I believe. That, in itself, may have aroused doubts in Dame Beatrice's mind.'

'Who can read the mind of a psychiatrist who specialises in tracking down murderers?'

'A single-track mind, you think. I do not agree with you there. She has something up her sleeve, I think. Perhaps when the next analysis has been carried out, we may know what it is. I have been associated with her as a Home Office colleague for several years now. I have learnt to respect her judgement. Anyhow, bring out your dead!' concluded Sir Ranulph, lapsing into incongruous cheerfulness.

'We shan't be called upon to identify father, shall we?' asked Morpeth anxiously, after the sisters had been informed of what was in the wind. 'I couldn't bear that, I really couldn't.'

'Of course we shan't be asked to do anything of the kind. What a horrible idea!' responded Bryony. 'Father's name is on the coffin. That will be sufficient identification. Nobody will query it, so stop worrying. I don't know how they will manage about the other one. He was buried before it was known that he was the Castercombe chemist's assistant. The cemetery people will have records of the graves, though, and anyway he is no business of ours. I take it very unfriendly of Dame Beatrice to have father dug up, but there it is.'

'I don't think it was her decision,' said Morpeth. 'Once she had voiced her suspicions they must have carried some weight, but after that the whole thing would be up to the police.'

'I loathe the business of digging people up when once they've been buried,' said Laura. 'We ought to leave the dead in peace, whatever they've done in this life.'

'Coffins are often dug up,' said Dame Beatrice. 'Sometimes the dead are honoured in the process. How would you like to be transferred to Westminster Abbey after you have lain for a period in a not very attractive local burying ground?'

'Don't be frivolous. That sort of re-burial is an entirely different matter and you know it. Not that one wouldn't find Westminster Abbey rather chilly. At least the local cemetery gets some warmth whenever the sun chooses to shine.'

'Which does not appear to be today.' Dame Beatrice looked out of a window against which the heavy summer rain, borne on a south-west wind, was lashing and streaming. 'I do not envy the grave-diggers their task if this break in the weather we are experiencing has reached Axehead.'

'Well, good luck to them, but I can't see any point in tomorrow's activities. Even if Dr Rant did die when he did because something extra had been put into the dope or drink he furnished for himself, there wouldn't be any traces left after all this time, would there? I mean, he's been dead for several years.'

'There is always our old friend arsenic,' said Dame Beatrice, 'and it is a treacherous friend to a murderer. It leaves long-term traces of itself in hair and fingernails, neither of which, in the grave, is likely to receive the attentions of a barber or a chiropodist, even a ghostly one.'

'Arsenic? Surely no poisoner uses *that* any more? I mean, it's so readily obtainable from all sorts of things you can find in any gardener's shed that anybody can get hold of it. It would be suspected and tested at once in any cases of unexplained death.'

'But Dr Rant's death was *not* unexplained. From what we have been told, he was, perhaps unintentionally, heading for suicide anyway.'

'Then why should anybody help him along by killing him?'

'That, as you would say, is the sixty-four-thousand-dollar question. There must be an answer to it and, although this is nothing but speculation, I think the answer may be that the Castercombe chemist, now deceased, may have been suffering from impaired eyesight.'

Laura looked resignedly at her employer, but then her expression changed.

'Ah!' she said. 'But that wouldn't be murder if he misread Dr Rant's prescriptions. The worst that could be brought in is criminal negligence.'

'The symptoms of arsenic poisoning are markedly similar to those of gastro-enteritis.'

'But that fact has been known for donkey's years! Somebody would have smelt a rat in Dr Rant's case.'

'Dr Rant's weakness for alcohol was also well known. That, coupled with his dangerous practice of taking a drug as well, causes me to think that nobody who knew him would have been surprised by his death.'

'We know that Dr Rant was unpopular with the villagers, but if he was poisoned it's unlikely that anyone outside the house was responsible. How would they have got at his food and drink?'

'You see where all this leads us, do you not?'

'Oh, yes,' said Laura soberly, 'it leads us straight back to Bryony, Morpeth, Susan and Dr Mortlake. They all benefited from the death of Dr Rant. The girls got their freedom, the house and most of the money, Mortlake got his own medical practice and Susan, although she seems a long shot, got the job and the companionship she wanted. Oh, I know the two sisters didn't take on the Pharaoh hounds until some time after their father's death, but there's no proof that Susan hadn't made their acquaintance and so heard of the plans they had made for when their father handed in his passport. She may then have made her own plans.'

'Susan, however, falls into the same category as the villagers,' Dame Beatrice pointed out. 'She had no entrée to Crozier Lodge until after Dr Rant's death, and therefore, so far as I can see, no opportunity to poison him.'

'There *is* something we're leaving out of our calculations, though,' said Laura. 'Wasn't there some rumour that Rant had inherited a lot of money from an old lady in the Midlands and was more or less hounded out of the place because of all the gossip and ugly rumours which were being circulated?'

'The same objection stands as in the case of the villagers and Susan. They may have had the means and the motive, but they lacked the opportunity.'

'I don't agree. The old lady's relatives, hopping mad at having the cup of opulence dashed from their lips, could have traced Rant to Abbots Crozier easily enough. I suppose he was in the Medical Register and the telephone book and so forth. It might have proved a longish job to track him down, but they could have done it.'

'Oh, yes, as you point out. What then?'

'They could have posed as patients and gone to his surgery. That would have got them inside Crozier Lodge. There they could have polished off the man who had done them out of the lolly. Ten to one he wouldn't have known them if they had never turned up at the old lady's bedside while he was attending her, so he wouldn't have suspected that any dirty work was afoot. Weren't we told that the villagers, in the end, avoided him and that most of his work was tending the sick or injured holidaymakers? He wouldn't have suspected a thing when this lot blew in.'

'You think of everything,' said Dame Beatrice admiringly, 'but you seem to gather your theories out of thin air,' she added. 'We do not even know whether there *were* any dispossessed relatives.'

'And we don't even know for sure that Dr Rant was murdered,' retorted Laura.

'As I believe I said once before, if Dr Rant was *not* murdered, my own theories collapse like pricked balloons,' said Dame Beatrice.

The fourth conversation had been held in the evening of the day before the exhumations were to take place. Detective-Inspector Harrow was in conference with Detective-Sergeant Callum. They had returned to the Axehead police station after they had superintended the erection of tarpaulin screens around the two graves and the digging operations which were the preliminaries to the work of the morrow.

'Even if we do find out from Sir Ranulph that both were murdered, I can't see how it's going to get us any nearer to finding the murderer, sir,' said Callum.

'Or that the same person murdered both of them,' said Harrow. 'In fact, on the face of it, it seems very unlikely that the same person did. The bank here has been very helpful and there is no indication at all that Rant had obtained any money by blackmail. Yet Dame Beatrice seems certain that blackmail

is at the bottom of this business and that the murderer, whoever he is, killed because he was being blackmailed. Even supposing that somebody poisoned Dr Rant a bit quicker than he
was already poisoning himself, we've found nothing to con-
nect his death with that of the other two.'

'Money must come into it somewhere, though, sir.'

'One thing Dame Beatrice has done for us is to produce this
flint object.'

'Do you think it will fit the hole in that fellow's head, sir?'

'That's for Sir Ranulph to say, but it wouldn't surprise me.
We've been doubtful about the verdict at that inquest from
the beginning, but, given the evidence, such as it was, I suppose the coroner had no option but to direct his jury to find as
they did. Neither you nor I, I take it, would have taken off his
trousers and thrown them to a dog to pacify it, but it takes all
sorts. Anyway, we're both convinced that nothing of the sort
happened. We've both seen the dog and Pollyanna could take
its correspondence course. It's almost indecently friendly and
couldn't scare a child of two.'

'Some people are terrified even if the most affectionate dog
jumps up at them, sir. I don't know which of the phobias you
would call it.'

'I can understand a child or a nervous woman being
alarmed, but not a grown man and certainly not to the extent
that has been suggested. The myth about the trousers was
unbelievable from the first and, very soon, so was the theory
that the fellow had slipped on the stones in the riverbed,
knocked himself out and was drowned before he could save
himself. No. Dame Beatrice may be dead right about one
thing. If a stone killed the chap, this could easily be the one.'
He picked up the neolithic dagger and looked it over critically.
'It fits the hand all right, although I think it would fit Dame
Beatrice's small hand better than it does mine.'

'She seemed a bit vague as to where she found it, sir, I
thought.'

'Oh, I don't think so. She said that Mrs Gavin went paddling and noticed that the thing looked different from the other pebbles. She admitted that they had been looking for it.'

'After all this time, sir? Oh, well, perhaps it wasn't the first time she and Mrs Gavin had been to Watersmeet to look for it. There's no proof it was the murder weapon, though.'

'She produced what she seems to think is double proof: first, that, as we knew a long time ago, there is no flint in this part of the country; second, that this is a worked flint.'

'Flint could be brought in for road repairs, sir, and this piece brought in along with the rest of the chippings.'

'All right, show me the part of a local road where such repairs have been made. Even if you can, it couldn't be any-where near Watersmeet. There's only a woodland path beside the river which leads to where the man died.'

'You will be showing the bit of flint to Sir Ranulph, of course, sir?'

'Of course. Don't ask damn silly questions. Still, as you *have* asked one, I'll give you a damn silly answer. When Sir Ranulph has done with it, I shall show it to the murderer.'

'But we don't know – '

'Who the murderer is? No, we don't, but Dame Beatrice swears she does and, such is her reputation, I am forced to do as she says when she names the murderer. Well, come on down to the Axe and Sapling and I'll buy you a drink.'

'They don't take axes to saplings,' said Callum, 'but it's a new pub and the landlord is a Londoner, so what can you expect?'

'His country lore may be all askew, but there's nothing wrong with his beer,' said Harrow.

The exhumations took their grisly course, beginning at five in the morning. The rain soaked down, the ground around the graves was a mass of trampled mud, and the only comfort to be got out of the affair was that the weather kept away even the most morbid-minded sightseer.

The two graves were a long way apart. Dr Rant's head-stone

had an honoured place along the central path through the cemetery; the chemist's one-time errand-boy had been buried on the outskirts and his grave was unmarked except on the custodian's map.

The little knot of men whose business it was to be on the scene waited in the rain, hats pulled down and dripping from the brim, coat collars turned up; but the heavy work had all been done on the previous evening when the cemetery had been closed to the public, so the time of waiting in the wet was not over-long and the coffins were soon on their way.

Sir Ranulph and the county pathologist were both present at what the former called 'the lifting', so were Harrow, Callum and a reporter (uninvited and outside the cemetery railings) from the Axehead local newspaper. There were also two grave-diggers, there to put the finishing touches to their work of the previous day and also to join with the custodian in verifying the information on the metal labels of the coffins. At the gates of the cemetery two uniformed constables had been stationed to ensure that no unauthorised persons attempted to storm the fortress of the dead, and in the street an ambulance waited to receive the newly resurrected doctor and the erstwhile chemist's assistant.

'Nothing now but to wait for the findings, whether negative or positive,' said Harrow to Callum as they sheltered in a shop doorway before making their separate ways home for breakfast. 'It will take some time, I reckon, before we get a report.'

'At any rate, our investigations, since we knew the identity of the Watersmeet body, have given us some satisfaction, sir. We've traced the man's movements to a certain extent. We know he emigrated and we know he soon got into trouble and came back here pretty well broke. That's when he turned to blackmail, I'll bet.'

'I'm not as well satisfied as you seem to be,' said Harrow. 'We didn't discover who the chap was. It took Dame Beatrice to work that one out.'

'We beavered away at the Australian end, sir.'

'Only with a lot of boost from our own top brass, and we could have done nothing unless Dame Beatrice had got a name put on the man. Thank goodness he didn't festoon himself with a set of aliases like the valley chap.'

'Well, when he emigrated he had done nothing wrong, sir, so far as we can prove.'

'That's true, but he seems to have made up for it since. Dame Beatrice thinks the chemist left him to make up the prescriptions when he could no longer be sure of reading the doctor's writing himself, and it's likely enough. Her theory is that our chap mixed the ingredients cheerfully enough at first, but then something about the prescriptions made him suspicious, so he must have kept them as evidence in case anything should rear itself up later.'

'He wanted to cover himself and the chemist, you mean, sir?'

'Dame Beatrice is certain that's all there was in it to begin with, but that when he came back to England he saw the prescriptions as a means of blackmail.'

'But Dr Rant was dead by then. He wrote his own prescriptions. You can't blackmail a dead man.'

'The dead man left two daughters and left them pretty comfortably off, remember.'

'Is that what Dame Beatrice thinks? – that the women were being blackmailed?'

'It's what *I* think. That older one, Miss Bryony Rant, is bright enough to have picked up doctor's shorthand from her father and I've no doubt she had access to the official pad on which the prescriptions were written out before the leaf was torn out and given to the chemist.'

'So, as she was in charge of the Crozier Lodge car, she took her father's prescriptions into Castercombe to get them made up, you mean, but the prescription the doctor had written out for himself was not the prescription handed in to the chemist? I thought, though, that we were told Dr Mortlake took over from Miss Rant in delivering the prescriptions.'

Strange and bizarre things are done in the name of science. Some are cruel, some repulsive. The clipping of Dr Rant's nails and hair came, to the lay mind, under the latter heading, but to Sir Ranulph it was all in the day's work. That done, the corpse was decently re-interred. The Watersmeet man was already back in his grave, for the fitting of the *coup de poing* to the hole in his skull had proved to be no more than a formality.

The shrouding tarpaulins in the cemetery had not gone unremarked although, with the break in the weather, they had been seen by few. The news, however, found its way around in the way news seems to do and it reached Dr Mortlake through the agency of the local tobacconist.

'Doings at the cemetery, so I heard,' she said. 'Don't do to believe everything you hear, though, does it? There's some as knows how to make a silk purse out of a sow's ear, whatever our grandmothers used to say.'

'A funeral, Mrs Wake? I didn't know anybody in the town had been buried. Who was it?'

'Not buried. Un-buried, if you take my meaning, doctor, and there was two of them, at that. All done secret, with screens around and policemen on the gate and everything.'

'Good gracious me! Who were they!'

'Oh, well, you know what people are! They'll say anything if it's a bit spicy. I was told it might be Dr Rant for one. It was along the main path and just about where he laid, but, if that was so, I reckon you'd have knowed about it, you being a doctor, too.'

'Where was the other screen put up? You mentioned two graves, I think.'

'That's right, or so I heard. The other tarpaulins was over on the Beestone road end, but nobody don't seem to know whose grave it was.'

The reports came through in due course and could not be kept out of the local paper. From there they reached the big dailies and there followed a sensational article in a Sunday paper headed: *How many other graves ought to be investigated?* Analysis of Dr Rant's hair and fingernails had revealed nothing, so there was still no conclusive proof that his death had been anything but accidental. However, the subject of poison had been raised and provoked much speculation. Perhaps the doctor's worsening condition could be attributed to a slow, systematic poisoning which, combined with the quantities of alcohol he had consumed, eventually proved fatal?

And so on and so forth. The article skated round the edges of libel, for, although he was not named, it was clear that the writer blamed Dr Mortlake for not having spotted what was wrong with his chief. The report went so far as to call Dr Mortlake's professional ability in question. The London readers of the paper were titillated; Axehead, Abbot's Bay and Abbots Crozier were enthralled, and some of the visitors were distinctly apprehensive and confided to one another in the hotel lounges after dinner how thankful they were that they had not been compelled by illness to consult so incompetent a practitioner.

Dr Mortlake himself kept a low profile, but he did seek legal advice. He was warned that in an action which involved the Goliath of a popular Sunday newspaper and the David of an obscure country doctor, David was unlikely to win, so he held his peace and went to Crozier Lodge.

Here he found only Susan and the poacher. Adams was there on the excuse of having brought rabbits for the hounds, but the truth was that he was there to keep Susan company. She had been invited, with the Rants, to go to the Stone House, but she would not leave the dogs unattended even for a few hours.

'What do you make of the news, doctor?' she asked, when she had put Adams, with his cup of tea, thick bread and butter and scones, jam and cream, in the kitchen and had taken a tray for herself and Dr Mortlake into the sitting-room.

'Well,' he said, 'I'm not very happy, of course, but I had no suspicions at all regarding the death. A man who was juggling with his life the way Rant was doing was bound to lose out. It happened a bit before I thought it might, I suppose, but he had been undermining his health for years, ever since his wife died. I came over to offer my sympathy to his daughters. It must have been most unpleasant for them to have to face the details of their father's suicide all over again.'

'Suicide do you call it? Personally I believe in calling a spade a spade,' said Susan. 'Murder is a very ugly word, but, if it tells the truth, well, that's that. I heard they dug up a second grave. I wonder whose that was? Nobody at the Crozier Arms seems to know.'

17

Judgement Suspended

Susan and Dr Mortlake were in the middle of tea, although the second cup had not been poured out, when the telephone rang. The receiver was in what had been Dr Rant's surgery. Susan excused herself to her guest and went along to answer it. It was Harrow on the line. He announced himself.

'We've been to see Dr Mortlake,' he said, 'but his receptionist told us he had gone to visit the Miss Rants at Crozier Lodge.'

'They're not here. Dr Mortlake is having his tea.'

'Keep him there. We'll be along in no time. Now the news about Dr Rant's death is known, there are one or two points he can clear up for us. And, look, Miss Susan, don't tell him who this call is from. We want answers straight off the cuff. This is a very serious matter and we don't want a prepared statement.'

Susan returned to the sitting-room.

'Only the girls saying they had been asked to stay for dinner, so would be later than they thought,' she said. She went into the kitchen to her brother and said, 'Get it down you and hop it before the police get here.'

'Police? I haven't done nothing!'

'Get lost, I tell you!'

'Oh, all right. Got nothing on *you*, have they?'

'Who knows? Swallow – and off!'

Adams obeyed her. He disliked meeting the police. She returned to the sitting-room and unemotionally resumed her interrupted tea. Harrow and Callum turned up just as she was carrying the tray back to the kitchen. She put it down to answer the door to them. She noticed, as she did so, that, although they had parked their car on the drive, it completely blocked the front gates. Sekhmet, Isis and Nephthys were inspecting it, having already taken a sniff or two at the doctor's car which was near the house.

'Excuse me a minute,' she said. 'With the gates open, they could get out.'

'Shut the dogs up, if you don't mind, miss,' said Harrow, 'and leave the gates as they are. We shan't be a minute. Where can we find Dr Mortlake?'

'In there.' She indicated the sitting-room door. 'He won't be expecting you.' She went out on to the drive and soon had the two hounds and the Labrador safely penned. Harrow and Callum went to the sitting-room and entered it without knocking. Dr Mortlake rose as they came in.

'You'll have heard the news about Dr Rant,' said Harrow.

'Dear me, yes. So it was suicide, after all.'

'We think you could help us as to that, doctor. By the way, can you tell us what this is?' He produced the worked flint. Mortlake took it and turned it over in hands which, in spite of his professional training, were slightly unsteady.

'Good Lord!' he said. 'I wondered where that had got to. It's the gem of my collection. I was burgled a few weeks ago, so I suppose the thieves picked this up accidentally with the valuables they took.'

'You have never reported a break-in, doctor.'

'I didn't think it was worthwhile. You chaps don't seem all that clever at recovering stolen property.'

'Reverting to the matter of Dr Rant, we would like you to accompany us to the station, where I can have a shorthand writer at my disposal. Your evidence may be of the greatest assistance to us in our enquiries.'

'The police station? Oh, all right. I'll get my hat.'

Five minutes went by before Harrow said, 'Where the devil has he got to?'

'In the bog, perhaps,' said Callum. Susan appeared as they

walked into the hall. They questioned her.

'He's nowhere about,' she said, 'unless he went upstairs, but I'm pretty sure he didn't. One of the treads makes a loud cracking noise. I should have heard it. Besides, I believe I heard the front door shut about five minutes ago. I shouldn't wonder if he's scarpered. Not everybody enjoys being questioned by the police.' Remembering their search of her cottage, she looked at them with little enjoyment herself.

Callum dashed up the stairs, but soon came down again.

'Well, he can't have got far,' said Harrow. 'His hat is still on the hall stand and his car is in the drive. He couldn't get it past ours. We'll soon catch up with him.'

'Not if he's made for the top of the cliff railway and has gone by the cliff path. You can't get your car along there and, once he's in the valley, he could hide for days among those rocks. You'd better let me loose the hounds,' said Susan.

Without waiting for any comments, she dashed out at the front door and bounded down the steps. The two policemen followed, passed by Mortlake's car and got into their own without waiting to see what Susan would do.

They drove to the top of the cliff railway, left the locked car safely parked and made for the cliff path. Before they were halfway along it, the panting hounds, all six of them, followed a good way behind by Susan, streamed up to them and passed them. Susan dropped into an easy jog-trot and said, 'He left his hat, so I let them smell it. They know he is somewhere ahead of us along here. They'll find him.'

'I hope they won't pull him down and savage him,' said Harrow.

'Of course not. Gentle as lambs. They will hold him until we get there, that's all.' She dropped into a walk. Realising that, so far as the hounds were concerned, there was nothing to be done without her, the policemen followed suit. They came to the end of the cliff path and to the steep incline which led down to Rocky Valley. Seated on the cricket ground below was Dr Mortlake. The six hounds were in an alert circle around him regarding him with the affection which, if they are of noble mind, the victors extend to the vanquished.

'Well, what do you know?' said Detective-Sergeant Callum.

'You go first, miss. We don't want the seat of our trousers torn out,' said Detective-Inspector Harrow, looking at the slavering ring of canine eagerness.

'So let me get it all straight,' said Laura, a day or two later.

'The floor is yours,' said Dame Beatrice courteously.

'Funny about the English language. To be floored means to be baffled, more or less defeated, as I understand it – comes from prize fighting, I suppose. Lots of our sayings seem to come from one form of sport or another. Batting on a sticky wicket, for instance. Anyway, contrary to being floored, to be given the floor means that one is free to orate and to produce arguments, no matter how long and how boring.'

'Riding for a fall; drawing a bow at a venture; that cock won't fight; the ball is in your court; to trump your rival's ace; to hound a person to death; to miss the mark; the dice were loaded against him; skating on thin ice; a sprat to catch a mackerel; to run with the hare and hunt with the hounds – '

'To be three sheets in the wind,' said Laura, grinning. 'Meanwhile – '

'Oh, I do beg your pardon. You were about to recapitulate.'

'Not that, exactly. I only want to get things straightened out. When did you know that Mortlake was the murderer?'

'It has not been proved yet that he is the murderer, but undoubtedly he will be brought before the magistrates and they will decide whether he is to be sent for trial.'

'But you yourself think he's guilty.'

'There were indications when Detective-Inspector Harrow heard the story told by Adams about finding an interloper in the Rant's garage loft. I thought it possible that the person wearing the long coat and the hat was Susan, but when we confirmed the identity of the dead man at Watersmeet, it seemed likely that the motive for murder was a lot more complicated than punishment for dog-stealing.'

'The verdict on Todhunter's death and the one on Dr Rant's will be quashed, I suppose, as a formality. But what about that hat and the piece of material that the police found at Susan's cottage?' asked Laura.

'There is no doubt in my mind that those two objects were planted by someone who wanted to throw suspicion on Susan,' said Dame Beatrice. 'Whoever did it was careless enough to provide a hat of the wrong colour that did not even fit her – presumably in the belief that, if anyone had seen the intruder at Crozier Lodge that morning, they would not have been close enough to discern the details of the hat. As we now know, however, the piece of trouser material did match the garment found at Watersmeet – and that was more incriminating. The police were certainly concerned about Susan's involvement, but they had no other evidence against her.'

'It must have counted in her favour that she reported finding the body and lost no time about it.'

'Possibly, although a murderer might have followed the same line. Well, the verdict stood and then the valley murder took place and about that there could be no doubt at all. Whoever the murderer was, he was an extremely desperate man. In killing the chemist's assistant, he had scotched the snake, not killed it. Someone else was on to him.'

'I can see how the forged prescriptions had tripped up Mortlake in the end, but who else had the goods on him? Not Goodfellow, and it was Goodfellow who got murdered in Rocky Valley.'

'Have you forgotten that Goodfellow was a very unsavoury private detective? I surmise that, when the prowler began to visit Crozier Lodge, Susan justifiably feared for the safety of the precious Pharaohs and engaged Goodfellow to find out what was going on.'

'Then he was the chap whom Adams found in the garage loft?'

'Oh, no. That was Todhunter,' said Dame Beatrice firmly. 'Let's look at the facts from the beginning. Don't forget that Mortlake knew Dr Rant very well. It is my guess that he acquired proof that Rant had been responsible for the death of that woman in the Midlands and used this to blackmail his employer – in the hope of taking over Crozier Lodge when Rant died. Mortlake was obviously an ambitious young man without the means to set up his own practice. Rant promised him some money, but would not change his will leaving the Lodge to Mortlake. This refusal must have given root to an obsession: Mortlake became more and more greedy and impatient. He even proposed marriage to Bryony, remember? In the end, he decided that the only way to achieve his ends was to hasten Rant's death – which anyway could not have been far off – by doctoring his prescriptions. Bryony and Morpeth would not have stayed long in that large house after their father's death, if it hadn't been for the Crozier Pharaohs – and Mortlake could probably have purchased it cheaply because of its unhappy associations.'

'Your powers of deduction never cease to amaze me. So Mortlake saw the Pharaohs as having ousted him from his rightful inheritance? Todhunter's reappearance on the scene must really have put a spanner in the works.'

'Knowing that Morpeth, in particular, was of a nervous disposition, Mortlake thought that a prowler at Crozier Lodge would soon scare the sisters away – especially if he seemed to pose a threat to the hounds. By stealing Sekhmet, he was sending a warning shot across the sisters' bows.'

'But Todhunter realised what was afoot and lay in wait for Mortlake in the garage loft?'

'Precisely. But he was not the thief of our hat, raincoat and doctor's bag,' added Dame Beatrice. 'He had no fear of being recognised – whereas it would have destroyed all Mortlake's plans had *he* been spotted by one of the sisters. Mortlake probably visited the loft on several occasions before the fateful meeting with Todhunter.'

'Well, I know you don't approve of blackmail, but we must give this Todhunter some credit for spying out the lie of the land and giving Mortlake a taste of his own medicine,' remarked Laura. 'I wonder what possessed him to accompany a murderer and a dog to Watersmeet that morning.'

'That we shall never know, I fear,' said Dame Beatrice. 'What we do know is that, with the removal of Todhunter, Mortlake's problems did not go away. By that time, Good-fellow was watching his every move.'

'Presumably he was not watching closely enough to have witnessed the murder at Watersmeet? Otherwise, even Good-fellow would surely have turned Mortlake over to the police. But he was suspicious enough to confront the murderer at a later date – and get himself killed in turn?'

'It seems to me a logical conclusion.'

'We still have no proof that Mortlake murdered Dr Rant.'

'In order to blackmail Mortlake, Todhunter must have kept the forged prescriptions. Faced with them, Mortlake will betray himself.'

'Yes, but where are they?'

'I do not know, but a visit to Adams' shack might be useful. I think Susan may have arranged for Goodfellow to lodge there. It would have been a sensible place for him to stay if he wanted to maintain a low profile. Adams is not a man to ask awkward questions – especially of someone who frequently gave him generous presents.'

'What about the Rocky Valley murder? Surely, if Good-fellow had made open accusations, he wouldn't have risked meeting Mortlake in a lonely spot at night.'

'I do not suppose any arrangement had been made to meet there. As I see it, Dr Mortlake must have found out that his adversary Goodfellow was living in Adams' shack. Knowing that the man had to emerge occasionally to take the air, he awaited his opportunity and one evening followed him, fell on him from behind, pulled his head back and cut his throat.'

'But why would Goodfellow have taken a walk to Rocky

Valley at such a time in the evening? I know it isn't far from
Adams' shack, but – '

'I have never thought the murder took place on the spot
where the body was found. It took place on the moor. I think
Mortlake left the body to drain off the immediate flood of
blood and then carried it to where the hiker found it.'

'This is all surmise, though, isn't it?'

'Certainly it is, but it fits the facts so far as we know them.'

Dr Mortlake was brought before the magistrates and, after the
hearing, committed for trial. A police search of his house
revealed Dr Rant's old hat and coat and also his 'black bag'.
Bryony was questioned about the contents of this, but was
unable to give a detailed list. She was obliged, however, to
admit that the scalpels had disappeared. Shown the receptacle
which Laura had found on the cliff, she identified it as having
belonged to her father.

In spite of this, the prosecution felt that they were on anything but safe ground with regard to the Rocky Valley murder,
although, at Dame Beatrice's suggestion, Adams was brought
forward to testify that Goodfellow had been his lodger and
that he had taken his usual evening stroll on the evening of the
murder.

'Did you not wonder what had happened to him when he
did not return that night?' asked Harrow.

'I reckoned he had dropped in at the Crozier Arms.'

'Was it not one of your nights to go there, too? I am told you
were a regular customer.'

'I was on the slate, not being too flush at the time, and they
wouldn't serve me till I'd paid off me arrears.'

'Wouldn't Goodfellow have treated you?'

'Him? Scrooge could have learnt a thing or two from him.
There was I giving him grub and shelter when, for all I knew, I
could have landed meself in dead trouble. When he never
come back that night I reckoned either as he couldn't find his
way, being too plastered, or else as he had welshed, owing me

money. Then, of course, I heard subsequent, as the poor bastard couldn't have come back, whether he intended or not.'

Mortlake, however, defeated justice and the law. He left a confession and was found dead in his cell long before he could face a judge and jury. The verdict was suicide. He had taken cyanide.

'He can't have been properly searched,' said the Chief Constable, when he heard what had happened.

'He was a doctor, sir, and up to all the dodges,' said Harrow.

'I'm not sure they did much searching,' said Laura, when the news broke. 'Anyway, however the verdict was to go at the end of his trial, he was finished professionally and he knew it. You can't get yourself accused of murdering people and, even if you are acquitted, expect a surgery full of trusting patients. How have Bryony and Morpeth taken the news of his confession and suicide?'

'With equanimity. The two men he murdered meant nothing to them. As for Mortlake himself, Bryony told me that it was an embarrassment to have him in the neighbourhood after she had refused his offer of marriage.'

'Cold-blooded young spinsters, aren't they?'

'More so than you imagine, perhaps. I am pretty sure that it was only a question of time before one of them murdered their father. Dr Mortlake put parricide beyond their reach.'

'Well, it seems that Dr Rant would have died from his own excesses sooner or later,' said Laura.

'I think Mortlake and the daughters feared it would be later and I am sure all three knew that they were to gain under Rant's will, and so cupidity, as it often does, settled the issue.'

'I suppose Bryony would be your choice of murderer if Mortlake had not forestalled her.'

'Impossible to say which of the women it might have been, particularly as it seems to have been Morpeth who did most of the cooking,' said Dame Beatrice.

Laura looked at her distrustfully and then observed, 'Well, perhaps it is easier to believe that Morpeth added arsenic to Dr

Rant's soup than to think of another doctor adding it to his medicine.'

'In his confession Dr Mortlake alleges that Dr Rant paid him very poorly, when it was obvious that the practice – and the Rants' comfortable style of living – would not have survived without his, Mortlake's, tireless dedication and personal sacrifice. He was pressed for money and was in debt. In the words of a BBC commentator describing the losing player in a game of snooker, he needed ''to negate his arrears'',' said Dame Beatrice.